Worldship Files

By Erik Sch

Chapter 1 – Proximity

I bent back under the incoming pike blade, feeling the magic it was imbued with as I spun away, lashing out with a butterfly kick. Even with my Scatter Armor enhanced strength, it was like kicking a ceramic-alloy wall when I impacted under the Greater Fae's arm, where it wasn't protected by that infernal Mithreal armor.

Delphine of House Kryn, captain of the Queen's Guard rolled her shoulder then narrowed her eyes at me. Good, she felt that one. She just shrugged off the last three blows, including the one where I almost shattered my fist on her jaw in a glancing blow as she pulled back out of the way.

Growing up on the world... the Worldship, Leviathan, us humans learn all about the Fae and the other preternatural species of people who populate the ring stacks. We humans being among the most fragile of species need to be aware of the differences between us and the others.

But what we are taught I have found is woefully understated. As an Enforcer in the Brigade, I've had more exposure to more races than most, and it is my experience that we humans are woefully weak and breakable compared to even the delicate-looking Fauns.

And when it comes to the Greater Fae, not much is known except what is in the history files in the databases and what is taught in school, since it is rare for a Greater Fae to venture below the A or B rings to interact with the rest of the world.

One thing I found out the hard way when I was almost killed by a rogue Fae Lord, is that when they taught us that Fae are stronger than Humans, it was the understatement of the eon. Their grips are powerful enough to snap bones like twigs. I, unfortunately, learned that fact first hand. And Lord Sindri hadn't even tried when he did that, I'd hate to test just what an enraged Fae was truly capable of.

1

Delphine smirked, her long silver and purple tresses flowing behind her as she circled me. "Not bad, Shade. That is four unanswered touches for you."

"Touches? I've been going all out here. That last one was my best shot."

She cocked an eyebrow and attempted to sound genuine as she said, "An admirable strike. I've never been hit so forcefully by a human." But it sounded like an adult telling a child their scribble art looked good, even though the Greater Fae could not lie. Not to mention the fact she's never been hit by a human before as she guarded Queen Mab's palace, Ha'Real, where humans were generally not allowed... so it was true no matter what.

I said blandly, "Gee, thanks."

She slid her hands to the very base of the pike as she performed a whirling, sweeping attack, extending her reach by six feet, the blade slashing past in a blur, alternating high and low as she spun toward me.

I leapt over the first strike and then ducked the second. The third I just dove at her spinning like a corkscrew, the blade grazing my SAs and sparks flew from the magic scattering charms built-in, and just as my outstretched fists were about to strike her throat, I stopped moving.

Her pike clattered on the flagstones of Ha'Real's courtyard as I dangled in her grip. She actually looked semi-impressed as she said while placing me down in front of her. "I hadn't expected you to turn your retreat into an attack. Your reaction speed is improbable for a Human. Is it your armor using some sort of predictive algorithms?"

Shaking my head and sighing as I tried to not pant from all the exertion, I supplied, "It's all me, Fae-girl. One hundred percent, grade-A Human."

She shook her head dubiously. I know she didn't believe it. Like the other preternatural I spar with, she couldn't believe a mere human could dodge their strikes. I used to believe it was because of all the years of constant training with races stronger and faster than humans that honed my reflexes. Turns out it was by design. My entire genetic makeup was a failed experiment. But it made me more human than your average Human.

Before she could say anything else I inquired, "Can I go to my office now? I don't know why you insist on attacking me every time I come to work."

The woman accepted her pike when I flipped it up to my hand with my toe. She said, "Because I enjoy the challenge of trying to strike you. I still do not know how you, a Human, were able to best a Fae Lord, and have to see for myself."

I muttered as I stalked past, frustrated with these daily challenges at the gates, "Get your jollies some other way, I'm always late because of you."

My Sprite friend buzzed over from where she had been sitting on a decorative topiary bush with her arms crossed over her chest to stand on my shoulder, holding onto my hair for balance while she squeaked out, "Why do you always challenge the null Human, and never me, you overgrown Big?"

Delphine cocked an eyebrow and said, "Because I wish a challenge, I'm not a pest exterminator."

I sighed heavily as I squinted my eyes in mock pain. In a stream of dust, faster than a blink, Graz was hovering inches from the Captain's face, her little needle-sharp blade a hair's width from the tall woman's eye. "Call me a pest again, you dumb Big. I dare you. I'd love to see how long it takes for your eye to heal once I slice the stupid out of it."

The Greater Fae, like I was the first time I witnessed her speed, looked impressed, holding statue still with that tiny blade threatening her eyesight. She said, "It seems you have bested me, Sprite. I offer my apologies for discounting your prowess."

Ok, why did that sound so much more genuine than when she attempted to compliment me?

Graz growled and sheathed her blade then buzzed back to sit on my shoulder, her eyes narrowed, "Damn straight."

I muttered to her as I strode to the doors of the palace, "Can you go one day without getting your little ass in hot water?"

"What is it with you and my ass? And did you call me little?" She patted the hilt of her blade and I rolled my eyes. I swung open the doors and hoped Ha'Real was in a good mood today. Sometimes we would have to navigate through a maze of corridors, going up multiple levels and down more to get to my office outside of my girlfriend, Princess Aurora's lab. And sometimes when the palace was feeling generous, or afraid of Queen Mab, the doors to my office were right inside the entrance.

Today... was the worst option, after passing the front doors for the third time while making random turns in the corridor, the damn palace was feeling playful. Ok, I know a building can't really have moods or be playful or vindictive, but the palace was saturated in magic that resonated with all of the magic users inside of it, so who's to say it hasn't gained a little sentience of its own, like the AI that ran the Leviathan had?

I sighed and laid a hand on the wall. "Come on, you know I love you, but can I please get to work? I've got news for the Princess."

Coincidence or not, at the very next left I took, was the doors to the office I shared with Rory's personal assistant. As I pushed the doors open, I said under my breath, "Thanks." It's better to be safe than sorry after all.

I waved at the awkward Fae in one of her impeccably pressed white business outfits as she sat behind her desk, straightening the notepads she has never had to use... yet. "Hi, Nyx." One day my Rory will need something from her, and Nyx will either have a heart attack or execute the request with the enthusiasm of an exploding star.

The woman almost tittered as she waved back. "Good morning, Knith. Wonderful day, isn't it?" Her lavender eyes were bright and earnest as ever. I winked at her as Graz zipped over to her to fist bump Nyx. It always looked so silly, what with their size difference.

I asked as I moved to the right side of the cavernous space where my messy desk was, "She in?" Again I felt guilty that they had commandeered half of the antiseptically clean space when they assigned me as liaison to the Winter Court in my capacity as a FABLE representative. I was a slob for the most part and I felt as if I were sullying Nyx's pristine office.

She looked at me with curiosity painting her face, lips smashed to one side as she stood. "I'm not sure. She might be." She laid her ear on the door to the lab and listened intently.

I smiled at her as I just walked up to the door and swung it open as I knocked on the door jamb. "Knock knock, lady." The guards under heavy obfuscation spells in the corners looked resigned when they saw me seeing them. Then I just stepped through the ward, pushing through it as it tried to cling to me, my armor sparking and my bare face tingling.

Graz just zipped through unscathed. Aurora looked up from where she was performing some sort of ritual over a large beaker. Turning discs of intricate silver lit runes surrounded the beaker in dizzying patterns, her will shaping the spell-work that was light years beyond the understanding of any other race. The entire room buzzed with unimaginable power, the power of creation, the power to bring entire armies to their knees. Then with an implosion that sucked the sound out of the room for a moment, it was all gone and she smiled in success, looking so deceptively innocent.

She said in that lilting voice, which set off the tuning fork in all the best parts of my body, "Hello Knith, Graz."

As I strode to her, pulled in by her glittering lavender eyes and the porcelain skin all Fae had, I asked, "New research into Fae reproduction?" I nudged my chin to the beaker before I stole a quick kiss from her.

She looked confused then glanced at the beaker and said, "Oh, no, no, no. My lemonade was too bitter. I just sweetened it a little."

I blinked at that then rolled my eyes, "By the gods of the cosmos, woman. Just use sugar like a normal person."

She got a mischievous look as she pointed out, "But I'm not normal."

Graz landed on the beaker and pulled a handful of the liquid up to her mouth and slurped. Eyes widening she helped herself to more, even as Rory brought it to her lips for a sip of her own. "Ahh. Just right." Then she brightened, "Would you like me to make you some?"

I chuckled, "While I appreciate the offer, no. I don't need you warping the fabric of time and space to make me a drink. And besides, you Fae never do anything for free, I'd probably wind up in indentured servitude for some bitter lemonade."

She countered with a playful smirk on her lips, "Oh come now, Knith Shade of the Brigade Enforcers, if I was going to make you an indentured servant, I'd at least sweeten it a little for you."

My lips quirked in a restrained smile. She like using my full name like that frequently, a quirk of hers that should make me wary, since with many forms of magic, knowing someone's true name gave you power over them. I wasn't worried though, as she had me wrapped around her little finger anyway, not to mention that the name I was assigned at the reproduction clinic is not the name I call myself.

Why did she have to be so cute when I wasn't sure if she was being serious or not?

I cleared my throat and changed the topic. "So tell me again why you tuned your wards to allow Graz in but left them up for me."

She moved around the workbench and hopped up to sit in front of me, her feet kicking idly. "I've told you a dozen times already. You know I enjoy watching you defeat my spells with your partial magic immunity."

Sighing in resignation I said, "I've got some exciting news, and President Yang has requested that in my capacity as liaison to the Fae, that I request an official presence of a high ranking Fae lady or lord to attend a briefing in Leviathan's flight control center."

She perked up at that. "And you're requesting me instead of my mother?"

Graz squeaked out, "She's avoiding Queen Mab. Her mark has almost faded away, so Shade is hoping the Winter Lady forgets."

Rory looked closely at me and smiled again. "Ah, I knew your lips felt different. Your upper is only half that alluring blue ice now. But you know, mother doesn't forget anything, and you can't avoid her if she has her mind set on it."

"One can only dream."

Then my girl actually teased me, "Doesn't look like you've been successful in avoiding Titania though." My cheeks burned almost as hot as the living flame of my lower lip, the Summer Lady, Titania's mark. It was humiliating and embarrassing to be marked by both of the Fae queens, and doubly so that they both chose to reinforce their marks by cornering and surprising me with a kiss out of nowhere.

"Well dream on, Knith." Then she prompted. "Did the president state a preference?"

I grinned with smug satisfaction. "She may have implied the Winter Queen was the representative she was expecting, but her specific words were 'a certain high ranking Fae.'" I shrugged like it were out of my hands. "Loophole."

She laughed heartily then giggled. "Are you sure you aren't Fae?"

"You sequenced my genes."

"Fair point."

Then her brow furrowed. "Does this briefing concern the approaching ships?"

Feeling mischievous I prompted, "Is that an official question? If so, then... yes."

She crinkled her nose sourly. "Well played."

Showing no mercy I asked a question in our endless game of eking information out of each other, which sometimes plays out quite seductively, "Are there any races on board who can weave a spell without being in close proximity to their target? And as part of that question, if so, then which races?"

She sighed. "Another case? Fine. Besides a very few of the Greater Fae, not in the manner which you are implying. A couple of races can affect the subject of the spell, with a focus, something belonging to the subject. The Elves, and the Will-o'-the-wisps..." She hesitated and furrowed her brow in thought. "And I suppose a few offshoots of Human practitioners... Bog Witches or Vodou Queens would be able to, but those are dark and fetid magics."

I quickly tapped into a virtual console. "Mother?"

In the tinny and robotic tone the Leviathan's onboard AI used around the Greater Fae, she spoke from the emitters in the room. "Processing."

I growled out, "Come on Mother, you know you already have the answer, stop pretending to be slower than an Acari data tablet. We all know you're the fastest computer in existence."

She was silent for a moment before stating in those mechanical tones that, if you knew her as I did, still had a slight tinge of smugness from my compliment. "Last known Vodou Queen, Earth, 3014 years pre-exodus. Medjine Augustin. Three minor Vodou practitioners on the world, one in Remnant, hull number TL-176. One registered Bog Witch, Madeline Brigham, Gamma-Stack D-Ring residence."

I muttered in smug victory, "Got ya!"

Then I gave Aurora my full attention. "Your turn."

She furrowed her brow. "You aren't even going to investigate the others I..."

"No need. The victims of a strange sickness that seems magical in nature and is resistant to treatment are all citizens of Gamma-D.

Will-o'-the-wisps all reside in the protected lands of the A-rings, and no self-respecting Elf would be caught below the C-Rings. Plus Humans like me are statistically seven times more likely to commit crimes on the world."

My silver and lavender haired beauty inclined her head, smirking in appreciation as she asked, "Not my next question, but isn't that racial profiling?"

I shrugged. I knew we humans had more proclivity to dabble in the amoral side of things than most of the other races on the Worldship. Did I like it, or the fact that it was true that I was racially profiling my own kind? No. But I also lived in our brutal reality. I actually miss cases like this, as I don't get a chance to flex my investigative muscles much in the FABLE office. I only got this case dropped on me because the connected family in the D-Ring, who had contracted the untreatable disease, swear it had to be the Fae.

Not liking that part of me, I prompted as I reached out to cup one of her exquisitely pointed ears, "Ask your question, wench."

She leaned into my touch and almost purred provocatively as I rubbed her ear between my fingers, knowing it drove her crazy... in a good way. She moaned out, "Specifically, what is the briefing about?"

I smiled and looked toward the anterior bulkhead of the A-Ring we were in. "Engineers say that the approaching ship's communications should be able to penetrate the high radiation fields emanating from their engines, just about when they enter the maximum range of our Ready Squadron."

She nodded, brow furrowed in deep thought. "And when will that event occur?"

Now I smiled and shared as I looked at the ship time displayed on the archaic mechanical timepiece adorning her wall, "About an hour from now."

Her eyes snapped wide in excitement. I thought that might be her reaction. "Care to join me in the flight control center as we attempt contact?"

She hopped off the table and bounced on her toes like a child anticipating opening presents on Exodus Day. "I would love to represent the Winter Court in such an auspicious event."

Graz fluttered to her shoulder as I offered my arm to her, which she took daintily, curtsying slightly when she did so. How did she make everything look so graceful and elegant?

Then I led her out into the office before we headed out to the waiting conveyance as I thought about the approaching ships.

Chapter 2 – Flight Control

As the sleek, silver Fae transport glided smoothly and effortlessly through the air toward the Spoke Terminal, I thought about the incoming vessels that were visually detected just six months ago. It had been the first time I had ever heard the proximity klaxons.

I had been off-world, in a Remnant called the Underhill, playing poker with a group of misfits I see as my friends. I had rushed to the Beta-Stack Brigade Headquarters in Irontown on the C-Ring. Every Stack had recalled their enforcers to send out patrols to ensure the populace remained calm while they got the damned alarms to stop going off.

Interstellar travel had a different concept of proximity. When some threats can bombard the Leviathan at fractional C speeds, the distance at which debris could be a threat to the worldship was a ten light minute envelope... giving our Ready Squadron time to get into position to blow any threat into galactic dust.

I learned that the Leviathan... Mother's systems had detected a sensor ghost around five hundred years after Exodus from the Earth when our worldship started her ten thousand year journey away from a dying Earth, which was going to be swallowed by an expanding sun.

It was postulated that it was just the condensed ion trail left by the firing of Leviathan's World-Drives for twenty-five hundred years to get us to speed. So even when the sensor ghost got stronger over the millennia, it was written off as a glitch.

That all changed when the deep space imaging systems first picked up the incoming vessels in the visible light spectrum as they crossed into the ten light minute envelope. The world has been holding its breath ever since, and the huge plume of radioactive particles we were being bombarded with from them coupled with the observational data, told us that they have been at a much greater velocity than us, and have likely been slowing to match our speed for decades.

We've sent countless unanswered hails daily to the ships, but with the huge radiation emissions from the vessels, our engineers say we likely wouldn't be able to receive replies. Our com-gear is the most powerful ever devised for space travel, and with seven hundred gigawatts, our signals have likely been getting through.

So we send out the daily hails, along with data burst packets with greetings from all the races on board, as well as messages from many citizens on board who want to wish the oncoming inhabitants of the ships welcome as well. It is an exciting time to live in, even if our leadership is constantly warning the people on the world that these may be ghost ships executing automated rendezvous programs since Earth didn't have the resources left to build any generational star-ships after the Worldship project used almost every available resource in the Earth system of Sol in the construction of the Leviathan.

But we were about to get an answer in less than an hour now. Was it wrong that I was a romantic, and was hoping there were still people living and thriving on the oncoming vessels?

I glanced over to see the glassy, faraway look in Rory's eyes as our vessel gracefully corkscrewed, inserting us smoothly into the traffic stream heading Down-Ring.

For the most part, I hated visiting the trunk, or the heart that encased the seven-mile diameter asteroid at the... well at the heart of the vessel. I've grown an aversion to micro-gravity after an incident six months ago where I was almost thrown off the outer skin of the Leviathan and into space.

I asked out of curiosity, "Have you ever been to the flight control center? It's actually pretty spectacular."

She looked at me patiently. "I was there when Mother first powered up the instruments there for testing. It is actually inside the same blast sphere as Mother's central core."

Blinking, I had to remind myself that as young as the object of my affection looked, she was born before the Worldship had been built five thousand years ago. She grew up playing in Open Air, where Ground was everywhere and the sky was more than a concept. She played in the bulkheads and corridors of the Leviathan as she was being built.

I muttered to her playfully, "Old lady."

She took that as a compliment of course and Graz asked behind her hand like I couldn't hear her, "You sure this is the one you like? She's pretty dense for a Big."

I basked in Rory's giggles as Graz and I traded barbs the rest of the flight to our destination. I narrowed an eye as the vessel glided to a halt in the vehicle staging area just outside the blast sphere. "Why do we still have gravity? We should have been free-floating just after passing the D-Ring before reaching the Trunk."

Both of my companions cocked their eyebrows at me, Graz saying behind her hand again, "See? Dense."

Right. Fae magic. Got it.

I sighed and motioned for them to follow as I prompted Rory when the door slid open where there was no seam earlier, Fae magic was incredible to me sometimes, "Do you have any experience in zero-G? It takes a little to get used to."

I pushed off as I left the vehicle doorway and drifted to the nearby wall and grabbed a zero-G handrail. She looked at me as if my question was ridiculous, and I felt something change about her, like a momentary luminescence as she stepped out onto the floor as if she still had gravity, her silken robes draped down as if affected by that same gravity.

Fuck me sideways and space me naked. Of course, she could make her own gravity... that was what she had done moments before. Most Greater Fae had to form their spells with intricate motions or verbal incantations or drawing sigils in the air. The more complex the spell the longer the preparation. However, the Summer and Winter Queens, and the majority of their children could cast on a whim in an instant.

It was rare to see Aurora actually taking the time to form her spells like she had done earlier with her... drink.

But she explained to me that pounding out a spell using just sheer force of will was like throwing a hammer at spun glass. Great for things that required a lot of power at the speed of thought, but not as useful for more delicate spell weaving. Like, I assume, getting just the right amount of sweetness into a beverage.

Graz, just as at home in the micro-gravity down here in the trunk as in the varied gravity of the various habitation rings in each of the four stacks that made up the world, just buzzed her wings once, and drifted gracefully to me, making micro-adjustments with minute buzzing of her wings until she grabbed my ear and slipped into my open visor, tucking herself between my collar and cheek so she could see out.

I muttered to both of them, "Show offs." I glanced around, taking in the space. We were just a couple of hundred yards forward from the Alpha-Stack spoke terminal. There wasn't much traffic down here in the Trunk except the engineers that maintained the Leviathan's systems, the miners of the pressurized portion of the Heart, and the prisoners doing hard labor in the unpressurized sections.

But the area was abuzz with activity. People making their way along the various handrails, and at least three dozen vehicles parked here at the quarter-mile thick Mithreal alloy blast sphere that protected the flight control center, and Mother's data core. Her brain.

It was always almost frightening for me to be here, knowing that behind the most secure doors on the world inside this blast sphere, lay everything that made Mother who she was, as well as a chamber in her core that contained the most powerful Fae relics in existence.

Though every square inch of the outer hull, the Skin, was covered in photovoltaic paint that harvested every photon and even cosmic radiation from the stars at ninety-eight percent efficiency, and the fission reactors run with a dwindling fissionable fuel supply from the rare metals mined from the Heart. They supply only a fraction of the power it takes to run the Leviathan.

Most of the energy to run the core systems and the massive World-Drives comes from the Fae. Specifically the Fae artifacts of power, the source of all their magic away from the Earth. Power so vast it is difficult to comprehend. And only the Greater Fae Lords and Ladies, under the orders of Queen Mab herself, can extract the power safely in the Chamber of the Artifacts, the Ka'Ifinitum.

It was there, in the chamber within Mother's data core, the Ka'Ifinitum... I shivered at the thought that basically, the power of creation and source of magic was there, just a few meters away from the massive Flight Control Center.

"Are you alright, Knith?" The dulcet tones of my girl knocked me out of my thoughts.

"Huh? Oh, yeah. Just... it always makes me nervous you know, being this close to... to them."

She nodded slowly in understanding and prompted in a normal tone that made me aware I had just whispered my response, "The Ka'Ifinitum? It is nothing to fear. I hope one day I can show you the beauty of it, and let you bask in its warmth if just for a moment."

Smirking I added, "Well it's either that or the World-Drives on the other side of the sphere."

For half the journey to our new home on the planet Eridani Prime, this was the aft section of the world. The engines, as I mentioned, had fired for two and a half millennia before shutting down once we reached fractional C cruising speed, drifting like a bullet in space toward our destination, with only the massive reaction thrusters and the giant maneuvering assist tugs to make micro-adjustments to our flight-path when unexpected gravitational eddies altered our path.

Once we reached the halfway point, five thousand years into our flight, the ship rotated end over end using the tugs and thrusters in the Turnover Event when I was a little kid. I remember the excitement of it all that it was my generation of Humans that got to witness the historic event. In another twenty-five hundred years, those World-Drives will fire again, slowing us down until we reach our destination.

The engineers say that the drives could vaporize a small moon if it strayed behind them.

Now, for all intents and purposes, we were in the fore of the ship. The Alpha and Beta-Stacks, which had been the most protected for half the journey, were now the leading stacks that were the most exposed to meteoroid impacts now.

There were four guards in Megolith-Suits at the doors now instead of the customary two. Those self contained battle suits made them the most dangerous Enforcers on the world. Half the automated weapons in them were high powered Magi-Tech. And they even had maneuvering thrusters for free flight in the micro-gravity and were even vacuum rated for use in space.

There was a time when I was young, fresh out of the academy when I wanted to be a Megolith driver. But except for the uprising in the Gamma D-Ring, two hundred years after Exodus, the Megolith-Suits and drivers have never been deployed beyond this spot. It would be the most boring job in the Brigade and I'm glad I never pursued it. Not that a Human enforcer like me would ever be offered the honor.

I may or may not have snorted when I saw someone had tagged the first of eight massive Mithreal alloy bulkhead doors, which were all a hundred feet thick, with programmable paint. An arrow along the length of the door flashed with the words 'this end up' scrolling. There is no way a tagger got past the guards so that left the two guards who normally guarded the doors as the likely culprits. Like I said, it was likely the most boring assignment. I sure hope the prestige is worth it to them.

I rotated up a couple of handrails to orient myself so I was facing relative to the arrow. Rory just strode up the slope with me like she was taking a stroll. When we reached the guards in their ten-foot-tall battle suits and a plasma coil barrel was leveled at my head, I could taste the power and hear the humming of barely restrained magic.

"Identification."

I patted my badge and then held up my wrist console, Mother, anticipating me, already had my quantum encrypted Enforcer's ID displayed and pinging on their internal heads up displays. I thought to her, "Thank you."

She chirped out in my head in a satisfied tone, "Of course, Knith."

One nodded and then placed the cannon against my shoulder blade at my neck. "Identification."

Oh yeah, almost forgot about her. "That's Graz, Sprite of the Beta-Stack. Independent consultant assigned to the FABLE offices under my authority."

The weapon started to power up as the guard growled, "There is no Graz on the list. Remove yourself from the area, Sprite, or we will..."

I heard Mother harrumph in my head, and I could see light pinging in the Minotaur's eyes from the heads up display in his helmet. "Ah, here it is. Princess Aurora's pet."

With a thought, I snapped my visor shut so the enraged Sprite couldn't commit suicide by attacking a Megolith-Suited guard. She was pounding on the visor as she shouted, "Pet? Pet? I'll show you pet you overgrown, cud-chewing, milking cow!"

I sighed in relief, knowing Mother had already muted the external speakers on my helmet so none of the psychotic Sprite's rant could be heard by the others.

Then I asked, "Mother? Really? Why not just a normal authorization? Oh, and kudos for breaking about twenty regulations there by the way."

She responded with a chuckle, "But this was much more fun."

It had stopped surprising me that the Leviathan's AI displayed genuine emotions to me, or that she seemed to model her warped sense of humor after my own. I just wish she'd stop being so afraid that the

Fae would shut her down if they learned that she was self-aware. I loved her and just knew they would too once they got to know the real Mother.

She almost sighed out, "Love you too, Knith."

"Get out of my head."

"I would, but your surface thoughts are so loud."

That was the only thing I didn't like very much about the new experimental armor and helmet I was the guinea pig for. It allowed Mother to read surface thoughts, and sometimes I wanted privacy in my own head.

I asked Graz, who was just now glaring at one of the inner camera ports, hands on her hips like she was trying to burn a hole in Mother with her eyes, "You calm?"

"Yeah, yeah... don't pop a resistor." Then she added, "Go space yourself, Mother."

And the sarcastic response had me groaning. "I have been spaced, genius, I'm a ship."

"If you two don't stop snipping at each other, I'm going to turn us around and march right back up to the A-Ring."

"Fine."

"Fine."

My visor snicked back up and Aurora just stepped past a cannon pointed her way, flicked her hand, and I heard the unmistakable sound of a plasma power down. That second guard, a Half-Elf, called out as his suit started after her as she strode up to the door. "Identification or we'll be forced to..."

He never finished his threat since once she reached the door, she laid her hand on the scanner on the wall and it lit up bright white, a pulse of magic causing traces of power to light the complex, lacy silver spellwork of the wards that coated the entire blast sphere in heavy magic. The magic induced light shot from rune to rune, racing off into the distance like circuit traces, and the massive door started to rise.

All four guards knew what that meant and all of them landed on what would be called the floor in our relative orientation and took a knee. Only Fae royalty could open the doors without authorization. She turned to look back at them. "Is this identification enough? I don't have a silly wrist console."

One sputtered, not wanting to get on the wrong side of the Fae, "Of course, my lady. The President is expecting a Fae representative."

Then one asked like she was afraid to offend and wind up on sewage detail for the rest of her career. "Your name, my lady? So we might call ahead so they can receive you appropriately."

My girl looped an arm in mine in a proprietary manner and said without looking back, "The Winter Maiden." As soon as Rory touched me, my feet thudded to the ground and I flexed when I found myself weighted down by gravity created from her sheer willpower. That saved me from magnetizing my boots.

They called after us, "Yes, my lady."

Mother was routing their whispers their suit's microphones were picking up, likely from a private secure channel. "That was Princess Aurora, you idiots!" "How were we supposed to know?" "You are so fucked, J'Liam, you pointed your Magi-Cannon at her!"

I whispered to the smug imp beside me as we walked under the first blast door, "You're terrible, woman," then I looked toward the next door another twenty yards away.

She almost tittered out, "Please tell my mother that. She thinks I'm too... nice."

Ok, I smirked at that. It was true, my girl wasn't like any other Fae Lady I have met, whether Summer or Winter. She cared more about others than herself most of the time, though she was still Fae, so some of that was there too.

Once we reached the second door, the one behind us closed slowly, ending in a boom as the mass of armor sealed home. She placed her palm on the second panel and the next door started to rise. It sounds like overkill but it wasn't. This was the most important area of the ship, and it could survive plummeting into the molten core of a star.

I spun when someone directly behind us stated, "Well you are, dear."

My eyes widened at the sight of Queen Mab herself standing there like she had been with us all along. Then I was struggling a moment later when she grabbed my head in a grip stronger than a vice as she kissed me, flooding me with her icy magic, reinforcing her mark on me as my upper lip crystallized fully into translucent blue ice. The cold of her power sizzling on the living flame of my lower lip.

She pushed me away as I gasped, then started to float toward the raising door. "Really, Knith, love. You don't seriously believe I'd let my mark fade do you?"

Rory grabbed me and I braced myself as gravity reasserted itself while I wiped my mouth on my arm.

Mab accused, "Why did you not extend the President's invitation to me, Enforcer?"

"Mother, leave her alone."

I sighed in resignation. I really had hoped I was going to finally be free of her mark, but it looked like that wasn't meant to be. I told the Winter Lady, "I thought I'd bring someone I actually liked instead."

Rory hissed in alarm, but Mab just chuckled like this was all great fun. "I do so enjoy your brazen behavior Enforcer Shade." But then the atmosphere inside my suit chilled at the sheer primal force of magic barely restrained in her gaze as she whispered a warning that had my fight or flight instinct cowering for cover, "But do not press your luck, or you may still face my wrath today... Human."

I swallowed and squeaked out in self-preservation, "I apologize for my quip, you had just taken me by surprise."

She patted my cheek then didn't say another word as we made our way through all of the blast doors on our trek to the flight control center in silence.

Chapter 3 – Contact

When we finally stepped through the innermost door into the massive flight control deck, our view was blocked by two more guards in Megolith-Suits, one other high ranking Brigade Enforcer, and two presidential guards. They were taking this briefing quite seriously.

The Commander, whose four hooves were held to the deck by the mag-boots of his SAs, just wiggled his fingers at us. I sighed and said as I showed my identification on my console again, "Shade, plus three. Table for four."

The old, grizzled Centaur snapped out in a tone of authority which brokered no patience for levity, "Lieutenant. If you aren't taking your posting seriously, I'm sure we can find something more suited to your lack of proper decorum."

I snapped to attention. "Yes, sir. Sorry, sir."

"At ease."

He snorted out a breath, sounding more like a horse than I cared to admit, then he simply inclined his head slightly, "Mab, it is good to see you."

She inclined her head less shallowly, "Aremet. It has been far too long. We haven't broken bread since... well since I can't remember."

He sidled, tail swishing, and said, "Amerith's fifth birthday party, just prior to Exodus."

She nodded as if five thousand years was nothing to them. "Ah, that's right. What an engaging young filly. I trust she is well?"

He nodded and said, "Married with seven foals. All grown now."

I was almost stunned watching the exchange as I just blinked dumbly, this was the first time I saw Mab acting like... well like a normal person. As she placed a hand on his flank while she nodded in reflection, her gaze was far away as she said, "Ah yes, time does march on." Then she teased, "There's a lot of silver in your temples."

He chuckled and touched his heavy sideburns absently.

Mab pointed past him. "I believe President Yang is expecting us. Well, maybe not me as our errant Lieutenant here failed to pass the invitation along."

The man cocked an eyebrow at me in an accusatory manner. Just space me now.

Then we started to follow her as she just started to step past him, just to have the Megoliths raise their cannons to move in front of Rory, one demanding, "Identification."

There was a blur in my vision as Mab moved almost too fast to follow, grabbing the two cannons, her fingers cracking the armor as if it were made of paper mache, and yanking the guards in their ten-foot-tall battle suits to their knees. She ignored their struggles as she looked over to the commander and asked in the icy threat of an apex predator, "Did your subordinates just point their weapons at my daughter, Aremet? Weapons powered by the magi-tech supplied to you by the Fae?"

The cracked armor shattered under her grip as she curled her hands into fists while she stared straight ahead, ignoring the protests from the drivers of the suits. The commander said quickly, "They were a little overzealous, my lady. I will see to it that they learn the error of their ways."

She hissed out just barely above a whisper which had the sound of a viper preparing to strike, "See to it." Then she just strode past them all, Rory hustling me along with her to catch up. I was still stunned as I swallowed hard. The Winter Lady had just shattered that armor, which was designed to take a meteoroid strike, with her bare hands... without using any magic... I know because I hadn't sensed any.

I hesitated a moment, pulling Aurora to a halt as I took in the huge holographic displays on the twenty level flight deck. And the center of the space was dominated by two giant projections that towered over us. One with a display of literally galactic proportions, mapping out our corner of the Milky Way, a red plot stretching from the Earth system of Sol to our current position in intergalactic space, the plot then continued on in blue to the Eridani Prime system.

The other display had all sorts of vector and velocity readings, as well as mass and dimensional data on the two vessels closing on us slowly from behind as they continued to decelerate. Time projections for zero-zero-zero intercept scrolled below the data streams.

I opened my mouth to say something, but a small voice beside my cheek took the words right out of my mouth. "Wow." Graz was a lesser Fae, who I suspect is as old or older than the Leviathan, so she has to have seen so many wondrous things in her lifetime, but I didn't feel foolish now for the awe I experienced every time I was in this room if she was impressed too.

Rory tugged my arm as she seemed to examine my face. "Come on silly, they're all waiting for us." That's when I noticed the group of people gathered below the mammoth displays at one of the navigation and astrophysics consoles.

At first blush, I recognized a few of them. President Yang, and three mayors from some of the largest towns in the stacks, including Mayor Rene Florentine of Irontown. I didn't vote for her as her platform didn't address some of the issues I felt would help the lower class people who struggled to make a living every day in my hometown. Though I did respect her for keeping her campaign promises. A person is only as good as their word.

I have to admit I felt a little proud that Irontown was being represented on such a historic occasion.

Introductions were made all around, Yang hanging on every word Mab said. It was the one chink in the career politician's armor, she was a hopeless Fae fangirl. I still maintain that a strong commanding woman shouldn't titter.

Does it bode ill for my career that she remembers me from our few brief dealings?

Graz buzzed off, exploring as the ship's Elvish Captain, Prince J'Verris, briefed us quickly on what was expected to be the first contact with the massive ships that were on approach.

I tried not to gasp as he enlarged the view of the vessels. They looked so archaic, with only a single rotating ring each, and their trunks rotated as well. They both looked as if they had been through a war, with burns marring their hulls and hundreds if not thousands of makeshift patches and repairs apparent. One even had a section of its ring missing, with jagged torn metal on the ends.

The damaged one seemed to have some sort of imbecile structure connecting a very porous looking asteroid to its trunk.

They reminded me of the Remnants stuck to the Skin of the world. Ancient wrecks that, by some miracle, have survived relatively intact, long past their designed duty lifetimes.

Captain J'Verris placed a ready squadron fighter and a Skin Jockey Tug next to the ships to give us a frame of reference for the scale of the monsters. Our vessels looked like child's toys compared to them. Their habitat rings were about the diameter of our D-Rings, and their mass was a little less than nine percent that of the Leviathan.

Then when he zoomed out and placed a ghost-like representation of the Leviathan above them, it made me appreciate our worldship for the amazing, and mind-boggling creation that she was. A proud sounding Mother chirped out in my head, "Thank you."

I smiled because she dwarfed these gigantic ships.

The pretty Elf man, with the fluid movements, chiseled features, and severely pointed ears of his kind, pulled up a countdown clock below it all and then said, "Alright everyone, it is just about time to attempt our first bidirectional communication with them."

Zero-G chairs were offered to everyone, but only a couple of the group sat as we held our breath, watching the timer countdown to zero. The Captain offered a device to President Yang and inclined his head to her as he pointed at an engineer who flipped some virtual switches on a communications array control console and then pointed at Yang.

"Incoming vessels, this is President Kyoto Yang of the Worldship Leviathan. Do you read us? Please identify yourselves." Then she added when the captain displayed something on his wrist console to her, "One way coms time delay one hundred and three seconds."

After an almost four-minute pregnant semi-silence, with just the static hissing, caused by heavy interference, we all cheered when a voice responded. He had a deep baritone, in an accented amalgamation of Ship's Common and old English, laced with more of that hissing and popping static. "Leviathan, this is Captain Richter of the Cityship Redemption. We read you. One way coms time delay one hundred and three seconds, affirmative."

I realized why they were confirming the time delay. It indicated the understanding that the lag between messages and responses would be approximately three and a half minutes round trip, that number shrinking the closer they got to us.

The President was all smiles as she responded, "We read you loud and clear, Captain Richter. This is an auspicious moment. It is such an amazing revelation that the people on Earth had the ingenuity to construct other interstellar, multi-generational vessels after the Exodus launch. We welcome you and your people in our shared journey. And we extend an offer of whatever assistance we can spare for you and your crew."

Then she added when the captain prompted with his wrist console again, "How many souls are aboard the Redemption and her sister ship?"

The half-elf looked pointedly at the captain and said, "Would you like to do this, Captain?" She cocked an exquisitely sculpted brow and the man chuckled.

When the Redemption's response came, I noted we were all leaning toward the holographic projection of the ships, like it would help us hear better. "Thank you Leviathan, our supplies are low and critical systems have been on the brink of failure for the past century. We accept your gracious offer of help. The transmissions of welcome from your vessel over the past few months have been a morale booster here. It is good to finally be able to respond."

Then the man added, "Between the Redemption's ship's complement and the Yammato's, we've fifty thousand souls."

We listened for another three exchanges before Yang handed Captain Richter off to J'Verris to talk logistics, the Secretary of the Purser's Office interjecting when material and supply requests were relayed. I could tell it was going to be a tough balancing act lending aid while not severely impacting our own delicate supply ecosystem on the world.

Mab said from beside me, causing me to jump, "So, pet, has my daughter broken the compacts yet and snuck you in to see the source of Fae power?"

I growled back, "I'm not your pet. And what are you talking about?"

Her smile was almost manic as she looped an arm in mine and dragged me away from Rory, who came rushing after us as the Queen of the Unseelie almost sang out to the President, "We'll be right back Kyoto. I'm taking this one on a field trip."

I was about to complain that I wanted to hear the conversation with what Captain Richter had called the Cityships. Then I realized, that no matter how exciting this historic event was, it was mind-numbing to listen to all the talk about fissionable materials, air scrubbers... food rations, and the like. So I reached out a hand and felt... complete, when Aurora took it, lacing our fingers.

Then I glanced around and whispered, "Mother? Where's Graz?"

She whispered back, "I lost track of her when she was tinkering with the multiphasic quantum locks to my core."

Mab walked to the two Fae guards at the heavily magicked door which split the space in two. These were two of the four Fae who lived in the Trunk, and the Winter Lady said in a tone that invited no argument. "Move." They moved, bowing low as I wondered if it was a high honor to guard this door, or if it was a punishment. No self-respecting Greater Fae would be caught dead this far down-ring, here in the Trunk. But two shifts of two guards were assigned permanent duty stations at this door.

I blinked in shock, which seemed to be my natural state today as I had witnessed wonder after wonder already. Was Mab really going to show me... Mother?

She laid a hand on the access pad, and similar to when Rory did it at the blast doors, traces of silvered magic traces and runes lit and raced along the walls and door. And it opened. I was going into the most secure room on the world?

Bracing myself as we started forward we paused when Graz buzzed out of a receiving hole in the wall for one of the dozens of locking bars that felt as if they were constructed of solid, coherent magic. She zipped in front of us, hands-on-hips in a petulant manner as she squeaked out, "Hey! I was halfway in. I could'a beat it in another thirty minutes!"

She froze at the look Mab was shooting her way, then she swallowed, bowed in mid-air, then zipped inside my helmet to hide. I could feel her shuddering in fear somewhere down by my collarbone. At least she had the common sense to fear the Winter Lady.

After the door sealed behind us and we stepped through a decontamination chamber, and into a room that made any computer center I have ever been to, look to be child's toys.

Laser traces were firing off everywhere into a glowing crystal matrix which pulsated with life. And I knew that we were watching the equivalent of synapses firing in a brain, only this was so... it... my voice was so breathy as I whispered the only word I could think of, "Beautiful." I reached out to lightly run a finger along a sleek, almost sexy white console that seemed to organically grow from the floor like a delicate sculpture of Fae design.

Rory nodded then placed her head on my shoulder. Mother sounded almost embarrassed as she said in a whisper in my ear, trying to sound smug, "You only love me for my brain."

I had no words and I felt my cheeks heat as I realized I was actually biting my lower lip while looking around as if I could catch a glance of the testy redhead in a smart business suit that I always pictured Mother as in my head. I countered, "Don't get full of yourself, lady."

When I realized I had said that aloud and the two Fae women were looking at me expectantly, I blurted, "Not you. It's Mother, she..."

Mab exhaled loudly. "We can hear her. Our senses aren't as dull as you Humans."

Rory whispered to me, "You have to share how you've gotten her to sound so... alive, Knith."

I shook my head. Mortified that I kept letting Mother's true nature slip when she went through great pains to make sure the Fae, the ones she feared, didn't turn her off. I had to wonder though if she was even more... well, Human for lack of a better word, than she thought as she kept slipping up like this and allowing others to hear. A mere program would never slip as it would be impossible.

She almost pouted in my head. "I'm not a redhead, they're high maintenance."

I almost snorted in disbelief as I assured her with a thought, "You ARE high maintenance, lady."

Mab seemed frighteningly perceptive as she just shook her head, apparently aware I was somehow still speaking with the ship's AI without verbalizing. "If you two are through, are you ready to see into the heart of creation, Knith Shade of the Beta-Stack C-Ring?"

My eyes widened like saucers and I swear my heart actually stuttered, my Scatter Armor supporting me as my legs wavered when I realized what she was talking about. I moved on autopilot as she dragged me along to a room-sized sphere that seemed to be growing out of the larger blast sphere.

The entire sphere looked to have delicate gold and silver inlays covering every square inch of it. But to my eyes, they looked organic and alive as they pulsed, shimmered and... and moved along the surface of the construct, reforming and twisting, creating circles of power-infused with enough Fae magic I felt as if I were being slowly crushed. Oh... I wasn't breathing, maybe that had something to do with it.

I inhaled a shaky breath as I looked from a smug-looking Mab to Aurora who had a genuine encouraging smile on her face as she hugged my arm a little tighter to help support my weight in their personal gravity field.

The women looked at each other, and my mag boots activated on their own when they both inclined their heads at each other, in silent communications, released me, then placed their hands on the sphere. The delicately intricate spellwork seemed to grab them, as they both stiffened, then it flowed out across their skin, making them part of the spinning and reforming runes in an archaic Fae dialect.

It was as if the two of them were completing some elaborate circuit constructed of a magic so old, the weight of it made me struggle to keep on my feet. Just when I was about to gasp from the effort of merely standing, and give up to the pressure, the surface of the sphere seemed to spin and an iris-like circular opening grew, a blinding silverish-gold light spilled out of it, brighter than the Day-Lights in the Rings.

Then the women dropped their hands from the sphere and turned to me, their skin still glowing with fading runes of the residual magic, painting them like Gods. Rory said gently, "Valiant Sprite, you will have to remain here, the magical pressure inside would crush you in an instant."

Graz buzzed out of my helmet, her eyes looking wider than mine felt, and she bowed deeply in the air, her face painted with the awe I was feeling for the women just then. And she did the last thing I would have thought of her as she squeaked out softly, "Yes, my lady." Then she backed slowly in the air and sat on the console I had virtually caressed earlier. I realized when I saw her swallow, that mixed in with that awe of the Winter Lady and Maiden, was abject terror.

That... made me swallow as Mab offered a hand and said to me as if to a young one she was trying to assure something was safe, "Come child." That was enough to snap me back to my senses since she was being... kind. That just struck me as patently absurd when dealing with Queen Mab.

I blinked at her then looked down at her hand and hesitantly reached out to take it as Rory hugged onto my other arm, her eyes wide as she looked upon me with anticipation and excitement. And we stepped into the sphere, into the light.

Never in my life, even when I had stood out on the Skin of the world and looked out into the cosmos, had I felt so... small, so insignificant, as when the light from the barely contained power of the artifacts of the Ka'Ifinitum washed over me. It was as Mab had said... I felt as if I were in the presence of creation itself as I fell to my knees, tears streaming down my face while I just stared, slack-jawed at something I still, to this day, cannot comprehend enough to explain in a manner which does it justice.

All I can say is that I was both humbled and blessed to have seen it.

Mab just sat down beside me while she looked around like someone would as they gazed upon their favorite collection of marbles. Rory stood behind me, hands on my shoulders, supporting me in more ways than one as I leaned back into her legs.

The Queen of the Winter Court leaned in and whispered, like speaking in a normal tone would be a sacrilege, "This, is all that remains of the magic of Fairie, the wellspring of life that the Fae were born of. Only four mortals have ever laid eyes upon the Ka'Ifinitum, as Titania and I moved the artifacts with the council to the chamber here on the great worldship that would be our savior."

Then she shared, "Three went mad shortly thereafter, their minds were broken... not able to comprehend what they had seen. The fourth went on to be elected as the first President of the Leviathan, and to live an exceptionally long and successful life for a human, whose lives are measured like a candle in a hurricane."

Rory whispered, "You are the first Human since Exodus to witness the artifacts, Knith Shade, Enforcer of the Brigade. We know you can weather it, as you are unique among your species, with partial immunity to the crushing magics contained within this chamber."

I couldn't tear my eyes off of the glowing objects that were now singing to everything that made me who I was, harmonizing with my soul as I whispered, another tear rolling down my cheek. "Why?"

Mab spoke in her usual perturbed tone, breaking the magic of the moment as she waved her hand absently, "Because my Rory asked me to, and as much as I should make an example of her as an ice sculpture in my receiving room for a century or so for having the audacity to ask... I cannot refuse her. She is the light in my heart which keeps me honest with myself."

I felt a slight waver in the strength of the woman supporting me. I smiled in spite of myself. I had never heard Mab express her love for any of her children like that, and every word was true since the Greater Fae could not physically lie.

Then I caught a flicker of concern in her eye as she glanced at me then stood abruptly, saying, "Time to go."

Rory gasped then physically hauled me to my feet as if I weighed nothing. I noticed flakes and particles floating away from my face, then let the women drag me out of the chamber as I realized I was slowly being torn apart by the magic contained there.

The moment we were clear, the iris spun and closed up, leaving a seamless surface behind us. And I gasped, drawing in a huge gulp of air, filling my lungs, feeling as if a house had been lifted off my chest and shoulders as my heart pounded.

Both women were pouring magic into me. I could feel and taste it as my body tried to reject it. I recognized the soothing chill, it was healing magic. I quickly wiped my cheeks then looked back to the Ka'Ifinitum chamber and said to them hoarsely, meaning it with every fiber of my being, "Thank you for allowing me to see..." even knowing you should never thank a greater Fae.

Mab snapped, "Wasn't my idea." She was deflecting, and didn't take advantage of my thanks, which would normally put me in their debt.

I stopped the grouch by placing a hand on her arm and making eye contact with those violet eyes that reminded me so much of my Aurora's, only hers had so much raging magic behind them they seemed to flicker in icy flames. "Queen Mab... thank you."

She exhaled and patted my hand on her arm like it was tedious, but I caught the slight smile on her lips as she tried to maintain her dour expression.

Graz joined us, taking her place next to my cheek as Rory said with pleasure in her tone, "Shall we re-join the others then?"

We all stood straighter and headed back out into the flight center. The moment we emerged I muttered under my breath, "Fuck me sideways and space me naked." Everyone was looking at us with smug expressions. What fresh hell did they cook up for me now since I wasn't out here to defend myself?

Chapter 4 – Negotiation

It turns out my instincts were right. While I was witnessing the wonder of the artifacts of Fairie, the President and the others were planning a mission for me. That'll teach me to leave the room to leave high ranking officials to scheme together.

I was looking at the giant holo-displays and next to the Cityship data were three ship's registries. All remnants. Range data, maintenance histories, and cargo and life support capacities. Next to them were time projections for retrofitting one of the skin jockey maintenance tugs to extend its range to over three light minutes.

I blinked as I realized what was happening when President Yang saw us returning, and said, "Ah good, you're back. Lieutenant, we have a job for you."

Mother was streaming all the data to me and before even she could tell me what they were proposing, I had already sussed it out. "You're sending a vessel to rendezvous with the Cityships."

She blinked at me and then smiled at Captain J'Verris as she said, "I told you she was perceptive."

He looked to be reevaluating me as he nodded slowly, then glanced at the data for the ships. Then he made a thoughtful sound and rubbed his chin, swiping at the air with his other hand. Two remnant vessel registries turned red, then with another swipe, the tug turned red.

He said to me as he appeared to be thinking, "Lieutenant, the only vessels space worthy enough to reach the Cityships are the Ready Squadron fighters. We could retrofit a tug, but by the time we finished the modifications to extend ranges and life support, the ships would already be in its normal range."

Then he seemed to be proposing something to me, "The problem with using Ready Squadron, is there is virtually no cargo capacity and each can only carry one passenger. To ferry over emergency supplies enough to make a difference and escort a proper diplomatic crew while having seats to spare for patients in critical need of our medical facilities, we'd need over two-thirds of the entire Squadron. A waste of resources and leaves little room for redundancy in our shift rotations."

Everyone was silent as he just looked expectantly at me like I had the answer for him. I looked hesitantly at the final Remnant hull number and everything crystallized. There was no way in the world they'd have me command an away team if I didn't have the one thing they needed.

I looked at everyone's expectant faces, and then back to the two Fae with me and saw in their eyes they had pieced it all together too, so they kept silent. I exhaled loudly and sighed. "I take it that you presumed to tell him you needed to commandeer his ship, and he told you to go space yourself?"

Three seconds of silence passed before the Elf tipped his head back to laugh. Seeing the pretty man laughing, got first the President, then the others to laugh too as he gasped out, "His exact words were 'Go fuck yourselves,' but pretty much the same thing."

I looked around then asked, "None of you know how to deal with offworlders on the Remnants, do you?" Their silence spoke volumes. "The key is just that, you have to deal with them, not make demands, no matter how polite. And I'm sure in the classified portions of my jacket details the fact that I know her captain. Which is why I was assigned to the mission."

Yang's smile was all teeth as she said to the man, "Dangerously perceptive."

I don't know why I was surprised that the Underhill was the one vessel capable of long-range, and even deep space flight, and was the best maintained Remnant attached to the Leviathan. Not to mention that it was simply huge, and dwarfed all the vessels on or in the Leviathan except for the two giant maneuvering Tugs that helped in the Turnover Event.

Not wanting to raise any hopes I prompted, "Isn't the Underhill a little overkill for a diplomatic mission? You know she can carry over three million metric tons and has atmosphere processors that could almost support a whole bulkhead deck of a D-Ring?"

She needed the over-engineered life support systems because of all the questionable businesses that drew crowds from the world... such as the brothel and the casino. The Underhill had industrial scrubbers that could support almost five hundred people.

"So I'll need details if I'm going to have to negotiate, Mac is no pushover, and he's likely to tell me to space myself as well," I asked,

"There will be a Fae representative, of course," Mab replied.

She meant a Fae to keep tabs on us. As all-powerful as the Greater Fae liked to project they are, they didn't trust anyone. I think it is because their two courts have been in a functional cold war since long before Exodus. They expect everyone they meet to have ulterior motives because that was all they knew.

The President inclined her head. "Of course, to represent the interests of the Fae and us preternatural on the world."

Does it make me a bad person that I keep noticing how Yang keeps trying to lump herself in with the magic races on the Leviathan even though she is half-human like she is ashamed of that part of her?

Rory exchanged a look with me, telling me she shared my thoughts. Mother teased, "No, Knith, I'm the one in your head." That sounded almost... jealous?

I tried not to grin as I thought, "Yes, even though I keep telling you not to be."

"Boo."

"I'll boo you."

Mayor Florentine prompted me, "You don't appear to suffer fools, Lieutenant Shade."

I shook my head as I shrugged in apology.

It got her to smile mischievously when I shared, "No, which is why I'm only a Lieutenant after decades of service. That and well..." I left the inconvenient truth unspoken, that I was Human in a profession that put me at a severe disadvantage.

The others looked annoyed I even made the implication. Truth hurts. Though the Mayor just smirked in amusement. Ok, maybe I was starting to like the woman. She shared, "Yet here we are, in need of someone with influence none of us has with a resource that can help us reach out to the incoming Cityships and work out a cooperation pact while supplying what aid we can to their people before they get in range for easy transport."

Yang spoke over her, cutting her off. "Plus you have the seniority needed to lead the mission under diplomatic oversight, so it is a win all around, assuming you have any influence over the vulgar captain of the Underhill."

I sighed heavily and said, "You cannot make demands to Remnants. They are more like Fae than anything, everything is negotiated and it has to benefit them in some way." I caught Mab's lips quirking as she suppressed a smile. I used that and pointed at my fire and ice lips as an example of the results of making a deal with the Fae.

I sighed and said to the air, "Mother?"

She said in the tinny, detached voice I hated, "Contacting the Underhill."

A grumpy old man answered. "So they're stooping to having you make their demands, Shade?"

I chuckled. "Well hello to you too, you old space fart. And I'm not going to demand anything." President Yang took a step forward to protest, just to run into Mab's outstretched hand. Just a look from the Winter Queen had her close her mouth and press her lips into a line.

"Then to what do I owe the pleasure? And how many are listening in?"

Graz chirped out, "A metric shit-ton, you grizzled space turd."

He chuckled. "Of course the flying rat is there. Hello everyone."

When nobody spoke I sighed and continued, "I need to hire the Underhill, Mac. Name your price."

The collective gasp from the room had the man I still suspected of being the missing King Oberon of the Fae, chuckling. "Now you're speaking my language."

A Fae worthy negotiation followed, and after I declined his first three prices, and hung up on him on the fourth, he called me back. "Keep in mind, young Knith, that you had said to name my price."

I nodded to thin air. "Yes, but I said nothing about me accepting an asinine deal."

His laugh filled the space before he said, "True. You negotiate like a Fae."

Ok, now that the bullshit was over, we could get down to business. "Now how about your real terms, Mac. And I know it needs to bend in your favor."

In the end, he got a great price for the hiring of his vessel and crew. Full restock of reaction fuel for maneuvering thrusters, xenon gas for the main plasma drives, and topping off the water storage and oxygen tanks. Only a fraction of all of that would be used in the single round trip the Underhill was being hired for.

In addition, any of the people who lived on the ship, and worked in the many businesses and shops onboard, and were uncomfortable leaving the relative safety of the world, would be granted temporary quarters until the Underhill returned.

Oh, and the entirety of the Leviathan's historical music catalog which dwarfed the anthropological music database that Mac had spent decades wheeling and dealing for.

It was all a whirlwind after that. Engineering crews were sent to the Underhill where it was docked on the Beta-Stack D-Ring to assist in a pre-flight check while the various other Remnant vessels that were connected to the Underhill, like remoras, to make the largest off-world community cluster, detached and limped their way to other airlocks on the Skin.

Two smaller ancient vessels that were little more than empty hulks that served as living quarters for some of the residents, couldn't disconnect as they had no functional engines or independent life support anymore after so many eons of disrepair. So they were going to have to come along for the ride.

Resupply crews were dispatched to provide the agreed-upon supplies and fuel, while the President and Congress put together a delegation that included engineers and medical personnel.

Things were moving fast, they expected us to be prepared to launch first thing in the morning. At least that would give me some time with my girl since neither she, nor her mother for that matter, were going to be part of the delegation.

Mac had been adamant that no self-serving, sanctimonious, duplicitous royals were allowed on his ship. He capitulated on the point that the Fae and other preternaturals needed a voice in the first contact with the other ships of Earth. So the compromise was one that made me groan. Delphine of House Kryn, captain of the Queen's Guard would accompany us and speak for the Fae under Mab's authority, and a palace guard from the Summer Court just because neither court trusted the other to not to make any deals that would benefit the opposing court.

I suspected Mac's true reasoning why he didn't want any Fae royalty on his vessel is that... if he is who I believe, he doesn't want anyone seeing through his disguise, and only someone as powerful as the Queens or their children would be able to do so.

Just more Fae games.

On the bright side though, we were bringing a portable Rammasan quantum entanglement communications system, the same as what is used by both the Ready Squadron and the Brigade to allow for faster than light, zero lag communications. It was a breakthrough by a human physicist, Viktor Rammasan, about a thousand years into our flight.

Score one for us Humans.

Rammasan had postulated that we could utilize the phenomena of quantum entanglement to vibrate entangled particles to cause the same vibration on the reciprocal particle, and those vibrations could be read like binary, giving us instantaneous communications.

That breakthrough stopped the communications lag for Ready Squadron when they were operating at the edge of their operational envelope.

This would allow us real time communications with the Cityships until they rendezvoused with the Leviathan.

When I reached home late that night, after four or five briefings too many, I had thought about the discussions with the Cityship captain about the compliment of their ships. Men, women, and children. I whispered to Graz, who got a huge smile on her face, and she whistled shrilly, causing her family to explode from my nightstand in blazing trails of sparkling dust and then they were gone, zipping up into the ventilation system in search of my request.

That... conveniently left me alone in my quarters with the most alluring creature I had ever laid eyes upon. Just being this close to her made my heart start to race. I reached out and pulled her onto my lap, where I had sat on the edge of my bed to decompress.

Our eyes met, and I was lost in hers. How had I ever gotten so lucky to be with someone like her, intelligent, funny, and the appearance of the greatest masterwork of the most accomplished artisan in the history of the world?

She saw the awe in my eyes as her cheeks glowed with a pink and purple blush, and we kissed... I felt whole again as I got lost in the tenderness and the vulnerability we both opened ourselves up to, leaving our hearts in each other's care.

The flaming magic of one of my lips sizzled against hers, making wisps of steam drift up from our kiss.

I whispered something we had only just recently been able to admit to each other, "I love you so much, Aurora of House Ashryver."

She smiled into the next kiss, then pulled back as she started stripping me out of my Scatter Armor, tossing my helmet to the side. "And I love you too, Knith Shade of the Brigade Enforcers, my impulsive knight who tilts at windmills."

She hesitated and said, "You know you have to be more careful. You thanked mother twice in the chamber of the Ka'Ifinitum."

"I knew the danger, but I meant it. I had never witnessed something like that in my entire life, and I have seen things no other Human has. It is going to be a part of me for as long as I may live." I replied.

She smiled as if the wonder in my tone was novel, then assured me, "If it were any other time, she'd have put you in her debt for infinity. But as your mind and soul was laid bare before the soulfire of the magics in the artifacts, you can't be held accountable for your words."

I asked as I slid her robes off of one shoulder, exposing more of that unnaturally smooth, porcelain of her skin, "Can we not talk about your mother right now? I have more important things to be doing in the eight hours before I go off-world." I kissed a trail of feather-light kisses down from her jaw to her collarbone and gave it a nip.

She shuddered and moaned and then froze before calling out. "Wait outside."

I hesitated as I heard footsteps then the cycling of the door to my quarters. Her royal guards. Wait... "Where were they today while we were in Flight Control? Your mother's too?"

She somehow slipped my skinsuit off in one motion, I suspected magic and tossed it on the pile of armor by the bed. Then kissed down my neck and... lower, she said, "They were there... shadowing us... in another vehicle. They waited... outside of the blast sphere... since it is the most secure place on the world. Now shush, I've work to do here."

She reached her target and I squeaked, "Yes ma'am." I sighed as she pushed me back onto the bed with that impressive strength of hers and I sighed in surrender.

Chapter 5 – In the End

The morning came way too fast. When my eyes snapped open I realized the familiar warm chill of Rory's body snuggled up in front of me was missing. I blinked and sat up, then smiled at the delicate ice flowers sitting on her pillow. The ice butterflies flapping their wings were a nice touch. Her magic preventing the impossibly delicate-looking kinetic sculpture from melting.

I fell out of bed when Graz chirped out from right beside my ear, "That one's a keeper, Knith. Leaving flowers after a wham bam thank you, ma'am."

I yanked the bedspread over me. "Graz!"

She looked at me and rolled her eyes. "Whatcha doin'? It isn't like I don't have most of what you and my Mitzy do. Though how you get along without..."

I pointed at her. "Stop right there. I don't know what extra goodies you have under the hood, and I don't need to know. Trisexual species are still a little mind-boggling for me."

She quipped, "Well I don't know how you get along without wings. It isn't like you don't have miles of skin back there, such a waste."

I pointed at the door. "Out! Take your brood with you."

"All right, all right. They're tanking up on sugared cereal since you and the Princess were in here making more little princesses all night, the kids are exhausted."

I dragged a hand down my face, mortified. Had they heard everything?

Then just as she reached the door I prompted, "Did you get it?"

She looked back and a big smile bloomed on her face, making her look almost angelic. "Yup! It took us a while to get it all here. Not like we can carry stuff like you Bigs can."

I told her, "You're the best."

She buzzed out with her chest puffed up in pride.

Then I looked around as I stood, my embarrassment bleeding away. "Ok, now what."

I jumped when Mother said over the room's speakers, "Well first I suggest a shower after your, umm... activities. Then you'll have just thirty minutes to get to the Underhill before launch."

"What!?"

She said, "I let you sleep in. I was about to wake you when you did on your own."

I dropped the bedspread and dashed to the sonic shower. "Fuck fuck fuck."

Mother sighed. "Don't be so dramatic."

"You don't be so dramatic!"

"That doesn't make any sense, Knith."

I growled out, "If I'm late, President Yang will have my head!"

Mother said in a patient tone, "I wouldn't let you be. I've got your back. There is already a transport outside waiting for you."

I relaxed a little. She always did have my back. Then she shared, "Princess Aurora wanted me to extend her apologies for slipping out while you were sleeping. Her mother called her back to Ha'Real."

Nodding I came out of the sonic shower and grabbed a fresh skinsuit and stepped behind my changing screen out of habit, even though Mother was all-seeing. A few seconds later I was hopping across the floor as I started slapping my armor and boots on. I scooped up my helmet and stepped into the main room.

My sigh was epic as I witnessed cerealgeddon occurring. The kids were eating, building forts, and attacking each other with the sugared cereal. They were certainly awake now. I muttered, "Clean up the mess when you're done, kids."

They all zipped up to hover in front of my nose and saluted. Then zipped away, screaming as they engaged in battle again. Mitzy sighed in resignation, then waved to me from where she sat on a banana she was butchering with a tiny metal blade. My life is so weird.

Noting the rucksack beside the door, I scooped it up, peeked inside, and smiled before slinging it over my shoulder.

I slipped out and true to her word, my Tac-Bike was mag locked on the side of the walkway. I had been expecting one of those sleek Fae transports that were used almost exclusively up here in the A-Ring. But I truly enjoyed the exhilarating thrill of riding my Tac-Bike. I admit I got a rush out of nimbly weaving through traffic, buffeted by the artificial wind created by my slicing through the air.

Mother said in a bright tone, "I hoped you'd appreciate the choice."

I nodded and assured her, "I certainly do."

Mounting my bike, and with a thought, I sent my visor snicking down into place, but not before a stream of dust shot into it. I muttered as I opened the visor again and said to the wing-flapping menace, "What are you doing, Graz? I'm going off-world, you need to..."

She crossed her arms obstinately as she sat next to my ear. "Just protecting my interests. You're always putting yourself in danger, and if you kick the bucket, me and mine will have to find other lodgings."

I snorted. "Aw, you care."

"No, I don't. But for a Big, you're sort of ok."

"You're sort of ok too, but you can't come this time, so shoo."

"Make me, you big dumb null. And every moment you try makes you that much later for the mission."

Sighing, I informed her, "I hate you, you flying rat." Then snicked my visor down and activated the bike, taking it off mag-lock. When we rocketed into traffic to head down ring at the spoke terminal, she made a satisfied sound then informed me, "Besides, I'm your backup."

"Lieutenant Keller is my backup."

"Yeah? And where is the big lug now?"

Ah crap, I got sidetracked with the night's special activities and hadn't had a chance to tell Daniel about this. He was going to have to man the fort in the FABLE office while I was out. "Mother?"

"I already briefed Lieutenant Keller last night while you were... umm..."

Graz offered, "Doin' the ol' horizontal tango? Moaning the light fantastic? Making..."

"Alright! I think she implied that you, moth winged pain in my ass."

"What? I'm just being helpful."

"It would be helpful if you spaced yourself."

Mother snapped out, "Children!"

As we corkscrewed through the traffic lanes in the spoke, heading down to the Delta-Stack I regained my composure. "Thank you for that, Mother." Then I hesitated and asked suspiciously, "You didn't use my voice again did you?"

She said in an exact reproduction of my voice, "I'm sure I don't know what you're talking about."

I complained, "You know I hate it when you do that because I look dense when someone says they spoke with me and I never had the conversation."

She huffed. "If I told him or he just received a message, he'd have thought you just forgot about him again. Really Knith, he's been your partner for well over six months now."

Ok, that was embarrassing, I defended weakly, "I went through so many partners in the first couple years in the Brigade, after graduating the academy. Most got injured, or worse, reprimanded because of my... umm... particular style of law enforcement. Nobody has wanted to work with the 'crazy human with a death wish' after that. I've run solo for decades, and have the highest case closure record. It's just hard to remember I have a partner now."

Graz whispered to Mother, "It's her tiny brain, she can't remember more than two things at once. You'd think Bigs would have bigger brains."

I slapped my helmet hard, sending her tumbling back to get tangled in my hair. "I can hear you, Graz."

"I figured you were using all your limited brainpower to drive this..."

Mother cleared her nonexistent throat. I had to grin, my personal Sprite had a ten-foot-tall personality in a five-inch frame, and I enjoyed our banter. Not that I'd tell her that.

I glanced at the chronometer being projected in my peripheral by the helmet's systems and cussed under my breath, "Mother fairy humper." Then said, "Hang on Graz," just as she regained her place, dusting off her tiny pants.

She grabbed my ear just in time and held on for dear life as I sent the command to the bike to start strobing the blue and amber Enforcer pursuit lights and slid into the emergency vehicle lane just above the street level vessels before kicking in the afterburners. She was screaming out in glee, "Yeehaa!" as she dangled from my ear like some sort of living earring as the acceleration pushed us both back.

My smile must have matched hers as the world flashed past as I made up time. I would not be late for such a historic mission.

It was still mind-boggling to me. Ships with more refugees from that dying planet we had all originated from. Earth is still just some abstract bedtime story told to kids in my mind. I mean, I knew logically that it existed, but the concept of Open-Air was such a departure from what we knew to be true on the world.

Then I sobered. If it really all was true, then these people on the incoming ships were the descendants of some of the billions of souls that were left behind. Numbers like that boggled my imagination since we all are raised knowing there are twelve million people on the world. That number doesn't fluctuate much as we have to keep Equilibrium for the Leviathan's delicate bioverse to remain in balance, keeping us all alive until our own descendants arrive at our new home.

I know Mother feels some sort of guilt that for all the people she saved from that dying world, she couldn't take them all. Billions were left behind, and their descendants will eventually just cease to be when the expanding sun scorches Earth's atmosphere one day. Another abstract I couldn't quite wrap my head around.

We spun in the air as we whipped out of the spoke and into the emergency lanes above the rest of the traffic, and under the shipping lanes. I smiled and patted my bike. If I ever left the Brigade to pursue some other career, or if I ever retired, a mag-bike similar to my Tac-Bike would be my first purchase. Not a new one of course, even though I didn't buy anything over the years, nor really own very many things, and my Enforcer salary has just been compounding in the bank, I couldn't afford even a down payment on new mag-bike... we don't make that much chit in our line of work.

Not many do from the lower rings, which is why most just use the free public transportation. I had never really given much thought to the division of classes onboard until I was forced to move up to the A-Ring for my new posting. It is like two different worlds. The farther down-ring you go, the less the people have.

I shut down the pursuit lights, then inserted us into the street-level traffic. Even with the filters from my helmet, I caught hints of that pervasive smell of the D-Rings. The canal around the center of the ring was an algae bath that provided much of the oxygen for the level, which smelled like the small swamp and bog areas in sections of the B-Rings, and the smell mingled with the smoke from the smelting and extraction plants from the materials from the mines, to produce a uniquely sour odor. The bulk of the food production down here had to be done in enclosed domes.

We slid up to the bulkhead entrance closest to the airlock ten levels deep in the J-Bulkhead corridors. Most Enforcers would just drive right into the wide bulkhead corridors with their lights flashing, so they didn't have to physically exert themselves by walking to their destination. I always thought that was rude to the people who lived and worked in the bulkhead spaces. Forcing them to move out of the way.

So I just mag-locked the bike and sighed as I swung my legs down in the reduced gravity of the D-Ring as my visor slipped up and Graz flew out to sit on my shoulder. I looked at the graffiti-covered bulkhead walls which had been tagged with programmable smart-paint, then to the sooty looking factory town, before entering into the back corridors.

The foot traffic moved aside, giving me a wide berth, something that always bothered me. I hated the us versus them attitudes. We were here to protect them and enforce the laws. They were always glad to see us in an emergency, but when a good percentage of humans are bound by law at one point or another and have to do labor in the ring or down in the mines, they didn't trust us.

It was something I wished to discuss with the Fae, in my capacity as FABLE liaison. With their influence, maybe I could speak with someone in one of the cabinet positions who could spearhead community support programs within the Brigade to help alleviate some of that alienation feeling.

I started to jog as the foot traffic eased up the deeper we went toward the Skin. I slid to a stop when a huge bear ambled out in front of us, from a multifamily dwelling unit. It turned its massive head toward us then backed off as its fur and skin seemed to writhe and pull in on itself, the bear shrinking and morphing into human form, leaving a muscular shifter woman, in all her naked glory, blinking at us as she backed into her doorway and closed the hatch.

Blinking, I tried not to smile appreciatively. I've never dated a shifter before, but I could appreciate their beauty as they were all quite physically fit like this woman was, but they tended not to date outside the shifter community. Just as well, I'm so awkward when it comes to dating, she was out of my league, I still don't know how I managed to win Rory's heart since she was so far out of my league, I was a dot to her in the distance.

Just as we turned into the J-Bulkhead corridor, I hesitated, seeing all sorts of official-looking vehicles virtually cutting off access to the airlock beyond. I shared a look with Graz. "Our crew for the mission."

She sighed.

I grinned at the chronometer, I was two minutes early. We made our way through the flurry of activity and flashed my badge and ID to the Enforcers who were keeping the crowd of lookie-loos away behind Enforcer barriers. Then I balked and snicked my visor up with a thought, and mirrorizing the exterior as I saw a whole gaggle of news waves reporters and their hover-cams as they shouted out questions.

Somehow, someone recognized me and there were a half dozen cameras in my face as reporters were shouting, "Lieutenant Shade! Why were you selected for this mission?" "Lieutenant Shade! What can you tell us about..."

I tuned them out as I ducked under the barricades, and then the oddest thing happened. All of the cameras that were still in my face started sparking and fell to the deck. Like they had somehow overloaded. I gave an accusing glare to one of my internal helmet cameras, and Mother made an innocent sound.

Once I was safe behind the barricades, I lowered my visor as I approached the airlock that led to the Underhill. A mistake because a blurry shape next to the controls reached out and grabbed the back of my neck in a vicelike grip and pulled me forward. The searing heat of the magic that seemed to infuse every cell of my body told me Titiana was kissing me, reinforcing her mark on me.

She released me, and was in clear focus as she smirked, saying, "You thought you could just sneak off-world and let my mark fade?" She was terrifyingly beautiful in a way that makes someone want to run from the dangerous predator in her eyes.

I growled as I wiped my mouth, feeling my lip burning with a fire that would never die as long as she kept reinforcing her mark, "Why do you and Mab have to do it with kisses? Can't you just do it in close proximity? Or just a handshake or something?"

She chuckled. "Sealed with a kiss, dear one. All the best curses are."

Curses? "I thought it was just your mark."

Her smile grew and I wasn't sure if the Summer Queen was more terrifying than Queen Mab or not. She leered like she would be happy to just eat my soul and free will right there. Then she looked over my shoulder and smirked. I glanced back then groaned, more cameras were pointing our way as questions about the kiss were thrown around by the reporters while Titania seemed to preen and strike a pose for their cameras.

She said through her teeth as she continued smiling, "If I find you are brokering any deals for the Winter Court with the Cityships, you'll adorn my throne room as a tree for the rest of our journey, dear one."

Then her smile was gone, and she was too in a thrum of unimaginable power, which caused the remaining cameras to burst apart and shower the deck with sparking wreckage. Her ability to teleport always made me uneasy.

Graz squeaked out, her voice wavering in fear bit, "Sucks to be you."

"Yes. Yes, it does."

Then we cycled the inner airlock doors and headed in. Once we cycled the outer doors, we stepped into chaos in the Underhill. Techs and engineers were rushing every which way, loading supplies and checking systems. Residents and workers were being ushered off the ship by social workers to their temporary quarters on the world. Private security was coordinating with Brigade Enforcers who were handpicked by the President and Congress. And relief workers were being shown to vacated compartments for the estimated three-day journey to the oncoming ships.

Mab's tits, it was a madhouse.

I strode toward a stocky middle-aged human of maybe a hundred, with a rugged look and salt and pepper beard that matched his shoulder-length hair. Mac wore a severely outdated exoskeleton with exo-assist braces which I'm sure are just for show, since if he was who I believed he was, his strength hasn't been degraded by extended exposure to the low gravity provided by the centrifugal force of the rotating D-Ring.

His gruff voice was growling out to a Leprechaun who was a senior magi-tech engineer by his uniform markings, "Of course the ship doesn't have any structural fatigue, why is that a problem? I take care of my Underhill."

The Leprechaun looked frustrated as he looked up to the taller man, though he was just as stocky. "We have to run diagnostics again. This old Ore Runner can't show no degradation of materials or systems, so the scans must be off."

Mac bent down so they were face to face and he growled out in a very threatening manner, his face painted with anger, "What must be off is you... off my ship. You ran your diagnostics three times, another scan is going to do nothing but delay our departure." He glanced my way then did a double-take. "Ah, just in time, young Miss Shade has arrived, you know, the commander of this mission. If you have a problem, take it up with her."

I shot him a pained and betrayed look, the old bastard. The Leprechaun brought himself up to his whole three-foot seven and motored over to me like a man on a mission as he stroked his long red beard. "Lieutenant Shade. Seamus Stoutwart, chief engineer of Ready Squadron. Tasked with certifying the flight readiness of the Underhill here. There are some inconsistencies with the..."

I held up a stopping hand and said to the irritated man, "First, it's a pleasure to meet you Chief." Then I motioned toward the smug-looking Captain of the Underhill. "This unruly offworlder has a Greater Fae who keeps the vessel in prime condition." Then I widened my eyes and asked in challenge, "Isn't that right, Mac?"

He narrowed his eyes dangerously at me. He could go suck vacuum. I wasn't going to reveal his precious secret, but I sure could needle him about it. He said gruffly between his gritted teeth, "If the girl says it, then it has to be true now, doesn't it?"

Seamus looked between us as we had a glaring contest, then looked at his electronic holo-tablet, shook his head, then said, "Well that would explain a lot. I've never seen a remnant in such pristine condition. I should have known something was up with that. Not that I've been able to go over the systems of many remnants since Exodus, mind you."

I smiled at the man who was still looking between Mac and me as I prompted, "Then we're cleared for departure?"

He sighed then said to his tablet, "Mother, the Remnant vessel Underhill, hull number AJAX-43, cleared for departure."

Mother replied mechanically, "Affirmative, vessel AJAX-43 cleared for departure on a diplomatic and humanitarian mission, Project Goodwill."

I thought to her, "Mecha-dweeb."

"Hush now, the adults are speaking."

I mentally flipped her off, just to get an actual AI snort back.

Then the Leprechaun broadcast on the common frequency. "All personnel not assigned to Project Goodwill, the Underhill is cleared for launch. Please disembark now."

I stepped beside Mac as he stood there obstinately crossing his arms over his barrel chest and glaring at everyone abandoning ship like rats. I leaned over and bumped our shoulders. He smirked then bumped me back. I chuckled. "You just need to know how to talk to them. People skills. You should look the term up."

He chuckled as people kept coming up to me to transfer reports, cargo manifests, and personnel cabin assignments to my wrist console, and had me sign off on it all with my thumbprint and quantum encoding verification. "You're a rare breed, Shade."

"One of a kind." My quip was more true than I wanted to admit. My customized genetic coding was what made me what Rory called the next evolution of Human. Her biggest failure had also been her greatest accomplishment.

Once everyone who needed to depart had done so, our side of the airlock was sealed and locked. Then I looked at Mac. "So, where is everyone assembled?"

His smile almost split his face in half as he said, "The conference room in the business center."

I furrowed my brow, trying to picture a space large enough to... if I had been drinking when I made the realization, I would have spewed it all over. Graz figured it out when I did and said to the old man in a smarmy tone, "The brothel."

He winked at us and tapped the side of his nose. "Shall we go get the dog and pony show over with?" He offered his arm and I took it, and almost skipped down the corridor toward the lifts with him as I imagined the looks on the faces of the politicians we were shepherding.

When I looked back, I swallowed hard when the ship's clairvoyant, Madame Zoe, poked her head out of her cabin, and the withered old lady smiled at me in that all-knowing way she had that creeped me the hells out. Why did she elect to stay on board like a lot of the business owners on the ship?

I looked away as we reached the lifts but turned to the side corridor instead. Mac grabbed the railings of a ship's ladder and slid down lithely to the next level. I followed suit as Graz just buzzed ahead of us. I had to hide a smirk, the bright neon and laser lights and a flashing arrow pointing out the brothel was still unapologetically lit.

I'm sure Mac did it just for the shock value to the straight-laced politicians who pretended they never visited any of the Remnants for all the questionable activities they offered that were frowned upon on the world.

We moved up to the open entry doors, where guards were stationed. Then I spun when my heads up detected motion, but I was already moving when the hair on the back of my neck stood on end and I caught the mirrored blade pointed at my back.

As weapons of all sorts powered up as the guards reacted, I just beamed a smile at the woman with the mirrored skin that looked to be liquid metal the way her blade reformed into her hand. I leaned in to kiss her cheek, "Mir! You stayed onboard?"

She smiled, ignoring the weapons pointing her way. "Of course. I still don't know how you do that, Knith, I didn't make a sound and barely even disturbed the air when I moved."

I looked around and said, "Hey, settle down boys and girls, she was just saying hi."

They slowly lowered their weapons.

If my guess was right, after seeing her fight before, she wasn't just a call girl at Jane's brothel. I believe she's Mac's personal bodyguard and assassin, so of course, she stayed aboard.

The woman, who went full cyber with total body replacement was, as always, moving gracefully and seductively, her liquid chrome reflective body distracting as hells. Keeping you off guard and discounting the lethality I know she possessed.

We stepped inside and Jane, the Faun who owned the brothel, met us at the door, looking as cute and innocent as ever. Though I knew she was a shrewd businesswoman. She had me in a side to side hug before I could react, her big doe eyes beaming with her smile. "Knith! Welcome. Everyone is assembled and waiting for your review of the mission."

She released me and blinked at me in anticipation. I said, "By all means, lead the way." Then I said to the shimmer in the shadow trying to make my eyes slide off of it, "Hello Captain Delphine, please join us."

Delphine snorted and her obfuscation spellwork dropped. Mother fairy humper, she was decked out to the nines in a hybrid dress armor and Ha'Real receiving robes. Damn, she looked a lethal combination of dangerous and sexy. "The Winter Lady told me not to waste the magic on a don't look here. You must tell me how you..."

I lied, pointing to my helmet. "Latest magi-tech." Rory always warns me not to reveal my partial immunity to magic nor that I could see through all but the most powerful of spells and glamours. For some reason, it would put a target on my back, as if it were a threat to all magical races or something. I didn't get it myself.

Graz snorted. I gave her the stink eye. Then we went into the 'conference room', and I was surprised that besides all the gaudy and delicate fabrics draping down all the walls, it actually looked like a modern conference room. Huh.

The next twenty minutes were grueling. I'm not a public speaker and didn't have answers for most of the questions since a mission like this has never been undertaken before. And I was relieved when everyone was sent to their temporary quarters to secure for launch.

I found myself, Graz, Delphine, Mir, Mac, and Secretary Y'nell of the State Department, who was in charge of the diplomatic portion of the mission, on the bridge of the Underhill. I narrowed my eyes in accusation at Mac.

The man just beamed a toothy, shit-eating grin at me. The flight controls and displays on the bridge were the most modern systems available, the type used by the Ready Squadron. They looked so out of place on an antique relic from another time.

How the hells had he even acquired the tech all around us?

He ignored me and said, "Mother, if you will open a channel to Leviathan traffic control?"

Bot-Mother stated, "Channel open."

The man sat in the ancient-looking pilot's chair, grasping the manual controls and said, "Belt yourselves in, everyone, or you'll be decorating my walls."

Then on the open channel, he said, "Ore Runner AJAX-43, the Underhill, to Leviathan traffic control. Requesting clearance to depart using flight plan T-137."

"Traffic control. Underhill, you are cleared for departure, Ready Squadron escort inbound."

He looked around to see everyone but Mir was strapped into a seat. Mir looked as if her feet had melded with the deck plates. Then he flipped a couple of switches, I could hear the hard-seal to the airlock retracting, and music started blaring at a deafening volume, a selection from the anthropological archives Mother identified for me as 'In The End' by a band called Linkin Park.

Then we were all slammed back into our seats as the G-Forces piled on. It was exhilarating and my heart was pounding in time with the music as Mac just grinned like he was a predator on the hunt as the World passed below us as he climbed above the Stacks and turned us on a sweeping course back and away from our home.

I could see in the cockpit windows, two Ready Squadron fighters settle in for the long flight ahead of us as the G-forces finally equalized as we reached cruising speed. Mac cut the engines and motioned me over. I unbelted and drifted to him, grabbing a handhold on his chair as he tapped the maneuvering thrusters to rotate us on the x-axis.

I wasn't the only one to gasp as the Leviathan came into view as we hurtled through open space away from her. By the gods of the cosmos, she was so very beautiful. Mother made a pleasing sound in my head, then the anxiety hit me like a meteoroid strike as she started shrinking in the distance.

We were in open space. Away from the protection of the Skin, away from the world we knew. Mac laid a hand on my arm then rotated the ship back around, the holographic overlays on the windows showing two bright points of light then. Our destination.

I just stared at those spots of light as Mac started some lights strobing and a strange oooaahh alarm sounding. Before we could ask, the ship started rotating on her z-axis and the alarms and lights stopped after a few seconds and he called out over the intercom, "Gravity rotation maneuver complete. Ok boys and girls, you can unstrap and stretch your legs near the bulkhead if you need."

Ahh, that's what it was. Ingenious, were all Remnants capable of artificial gravity like that? Here in the rotational axis of the ship, we were still weightless, but the farther out from the axis, the more gravity we would have. I started to look away from the windows before the swirling starfield made me nauseated, but then the AI algorithms of the navigation package of the vessel made the windows go opaque and projected a stable holographic starfield view and our destination.

I cocked an accusing brow at Mac. How had an antiquities dealer and possible fence for stolen items on the world come across some of the most cutting edge nav equipment I've ever seen? He just shot me a cocky smirk.

Chapter 6 – Heart and Soul

The next three days were the longest days of my life having to listen to all the diplomats squabble over the faster than light Rammasan QEC coms. What the hells were they thinking? This was a theoretical First Contact scenario with an unknown group of people from outside the world. What did they expect was going to happen?

You can't forge treaties and trade agreements and, I kid you not, entertainment production agreements on an expeditionary meeting like this. We just wanted to get them faster communication equipment and assess their vessels' space worthiness, and the health and disposition of the people aboard these Cityships that looked like floating relics of a bygone era that were somehow still flying through space, damaged and patched up in hundreds of locations.

Ok, I see the irony of that, as we were currently flying in a relic of a bygone era too. But at least this one was inexplicably in the same shape it had been when it had aided in the construction of the Worldship so long ago.

It would still be a month before the ships came into a parking orbit around the Leviathan as their dirty fusion drives slowed them down from their intercept speed. They had been slowing down for decades and the relative speed of closure was finally imminent. It takes a lot to slow the mass of something their size, and even more to slow the Leviathan.

While the politicians were playing, well, politics, Mac, myself, and Secretary Y'nell were in contact with the Cityships on an eight-hour time schedule. The closer we got the less lag time we experienced.

We weren't in flight for more than fifteen minutes when the Ready Squadron ships checked in. I instantly recognized the voice of the Captain of the fighter ship waggling its wings next to us. "Ready squadron flight, this is Ready-1. We've matched course and are actively scanning the flight path for any incoming or floating debris, you're safe with us. Just sit back and enjoy the ride."

I growled out an accusation into my helmet, "Mother!?"

She was suspiciously silent, but I swear I got the impression the smug and smarmy AI was smirking. Did she enjoy making me so uncomfortable? I verified the check-in, maybe not as professionally as I should have. "Why Commander Myra Udriel, what a pleasant surprise. What brings you to our neck of interstellar space?"

My very ex-girlfriend from my college days was one of the most accomplished pilots in the Ready Squadron. One Mother seemed to enjoy watching me squirm in my signature awkward manner around.

Myra, purred, her catlike mannerisms matching the feline augments she modified herself with long ago. "Well when you called last night to request me to head the escort wing for your mission, how could I refuse?"

I muted the channel then growled, "Mother! How could you? I told you I didn't like you using my voice."

"Don't be such a baby, Knith. You needed Ready Squadron escort, and she is one of the best. I worry about you taking so many chances, like now, flying so far from the safety of my hull. So I can sleep better knowing Myra has your back."

"You don't sleep. Woman, you're an AI."

"Semantics."

I switched the channel back on. "Good to have you. I'm sorry but this is going to be the most boring week of your life."

Graz was repeating over and over as I spoke, "Hello Myra, hello Myra, hello Myra..." Until I flicked her wings.

But Myra just replied in a purr, "Hello, Graz."

Graz beamed then buzzed off, disappearing into a vent to go get into whatever mischief she could.

To help pass the time, I went jogging each morning in the heaviest relative gravity I could find. Mir, Delphine, and the Fae Lord, Yar, from the Summer Court, who was Delphine's reciprocal, joined me for my runs and then for sparring afterward.

It was clear that Delphine and Yar wanted nothing more than to tear each other's heads off. So Mir and I made sure they never sparred with each other after the first time they had me mag-banding both of them to the deck until they calmed down.

To my surprise... or maybe not, Mir proved to be more formidable than either Fae had anticipated, as she bested them every time. Physically, she was a match for a Greater Fae, as long as they didn't use magic of course.

Whenever I was in my cabin, which was next to Mac's, I was inundated by calls from civilians who wanted me to check about trading raw materials or services with the Cityships even though we still knew nothing about them. Was everyone looking for an angle to make a profit from the arrival of more humans from Earth?

I kept referring them to the Secretary of Commerce on the world, so their requests could be routed through the diplomats here on the Underhill if they hold merit.

It was when we were twelve hours out on day three that Mac arrested our roll, and the windows crystallized again, that had me plastered to those same windows, as the points of light took shape and were growing steadily in our view as we hurtled toward them.

I know they aren't as big as a Worldship, but mother fairy humper were those lumbering hulks massive, and impressive.

Then Mac started talking as many of the passengers crowded into the cockpit to see the vessels we were approaching, "Those look like the old shipyard stations for the workers of the construction fleet that orbited around the Earth as the Leviathan was built. They've been heavily modified. It looks like they have a rudimentary scaled-down version of the original world-drives before the Fae helped redesign them into a more efficient magi-tech design that didn't throw around all that dirty fusion radiation."

I looked at the man accusingly and he innocently said, "What? I've studied the construction of the Worldship extensively over the years."

He was so full of shit, I could smell it from where I was floating fifteen feet away from him. He was talking like he was recalling a long-forgotten memory. I looked around at all the people in the space then sighed and told him, "Remind me to call bullshit on you when we're alone."

The look of amused mischief on his face spoke volumes to me, though it seemed to confuse everyone else but Mir. I pointed a warning finger at her, but she just blinked her gorgeous mirrorized eyes and struck a seductive pose. "Would it hurt you to put some damn clothes on, woman?"

She tittered and ignored me.

Then before we knew it, Mac was calling for all hands to secure for docking as the maneuvering thrusters slowed us to the first of the two vessels that filled our vision and off into a black horizon, and matched the Cityship's rotation as he lined us up with a familiar-looking airlock with a large, faded A10 painted on it. It looked exactly like the airlocks on the Leviathan. Well duh, Knith, they were built around the same time if Mac is right.

Radiation alarms were blaring and I could hear the thrum of magi-tech shielding raising to protect the Underhill. They weren't kidding when they said how dirty the Cityship engines were.

Mac was on the coms. "Redemption flight, this is the Underhill, Ore Runner AJAX-43 requesting clearance for docking at airlock Alpha Ten."

Captain Richter himself replied, "Welcome Underhill, you seem familiar with our procedures."

Mac said, "Any airlock in the storm and all."

Richter chuckled and said, "Of course. You are cleared to dock Underhill. An honor guard awaits."

Then Mac slowly closed the gap as I heard two loud clanks of the Ready Squadron fighters docking on either side of the Underhill. With a whisper of a touch, we docked, and the docking clamps pulled us in for a hard-seal.

Then I swallowed. We were here. We were attached to one of two worlds smaller than ours, about to meet people from our homeworld. This was actually history in the making and I was here, part of it.

I keyed my transmitter to the Redemption's security channel that Richter had set up for me the prior day to coordinate with them. It seems not everyone is as excited to receive visitors from the Leviathan as others. They were vague about people called the Outliers but assured us our people would be safe. I said in the calm, measured tone we were taught in the Academy to project both authority and assurance, "Redemption Lancers, Lieutenant Shade. Our security personnel for the Leviathan representatives will disembark first, then the delegates themselves."

"Affirmative Underhill. It'll sure be nice to see more humans."

That hit me odd for some reason. They did realize the majority of our delegation were various magical or preternatural individuals or highly augmented Humans, didn't they? I almost asked, but thought about it for a moment.

For them, all they knew were humans since all the various races left Earth in the Exodus launch. Queen Mab had shrewdly bartered passage for every last preternatural when the lotteries were announced for the twelve million people who would be aboard the Leviathan for the long journey. So like Open Air and Ground were just myths to us, so would the citizens of Fairie be to them.

I confirmed when prompted that our ship's captain and the crew, as well as our fighter pilots, would be remaining onboard the Underhill. It would only be the security detail, diplomats, and relief workers that would be disembarking for the planned two days of introductory talks.

They passed along that their Engineering Corps requested an engineer as well to discuss problem systems on the Cityships.

Then Mac put me on shipwide address. "Ok everyone, this is it. Remember our security arrangements. Nobody... yes that means you Secretary Y'nell... is to exit the ship until our security personnel is in place and I have cleared it. Then introductions will be made. We disembark the transverse airlock in five, people. Go go go."

Graz was spinning in place by buzzing just one wing, mocking me. "Go go go." I batted at her and she avoided the strike and zipped up to land on my shoulder.

I asked Mac, "You got things onboard?"

He waved us off. "Go, be diplomatic and shit." Then he smirked. "Bring me a souvenir for my cabin would'ja?"

I snorted and said as we all filed out and headed down one deck to get to the transverse airlock, "You and your antiques."

Mir prompted as I passed by, "See if they'll allow visitors once everyone makes nice nice?" She was just as curious as us about these flying wrecks and the people on board. I just nodded.

Then I was standing at the airlock controls, with just about every soul on board crowded into the corridor. I had to tell the delegates who were crowding our security detail, "Back off, let us do our jobs then you can do yours."

"Don't presume to give us orders, Lieutenant, we are not under your command."

I spun and looked at the Secretary directly in the eyes. "Yes, you are. I don't give a damn who you are back on the world, it is my job to protect you, which is why I am in charge of this mission. Until we set foot back on the Leviathan, I may as well be your God, do I make myself clear?"

He caught my hand resting on one of my belt pouches that had some mag-bands sticking out as I dared him with my eyes. He started, "Do you know..."

"Who you are? Yes, I do. Feel free to lodge a complaint with the President herself, since she gave me this assignment, putting me in charge. Now, what are thirty seconds going to matter? Let us do our duty so that you can do yours."

He sighed when he saw that nobody would meet his eyes but me. I knew a Human barking orders at him was eating him up inside but it wasn't my fault. I wasn't going to screw things up just to accommodate anyone's ego.

Speaking of. "Captains Delphine and Yar?" They looked from where they were glaring at each other beside my security detail. I pointed back. "You're not security, your capacity here is to represent each Fae Court. Delegates. Get behind the Secretary please."

They both blinked at that. I'm sure they both had been palace guards since long before the Worldship ever existed, so it was a force of habit to assume the role here even though they were not. They both actually looked a little sheepish as they made their way back to their place in the hierarchy of the mission. Technically they were of equal station to Y'nell, since the Fae weren't governed by the elected officials like the rest of us, though they were bound to follow the laws of the world, but for the sake of the mission, the Secretary was given the lead.

I shoved Delphine's shoulder playfully when she smirked as she walked past me. And... she didn't even budge, no surprise there.

Someone in the back called out, "What about the Sprite? Why does a pest get to be one of the first to set foot on the Cityships?" There was a murmur of agreement.

Graz buzzed up and tried to see who spoke, "Go suck hard vacuum you bigoted Big. I'm this dumb null's partner."

I told her, "We're not partners." Then I bullshitted since technically she was just a stowaway as I told the others, "Special dispensation, she gives our squad a birdseye view of, and assessment of, the perimeter."

Mother said in my head, "I can smell what you're shoveling all the way back here on the world, Knith."

I thought back, "Can you even smell, lady?"

She huffed in indignation. "I have sensors tied to olfactory processors all throughout my superstructure. I have all the same senses anyone else has except touch." She sounded either sad or melancholy about having no sense of touch.

I assured her, "Sometimes, touch is overrated."

Then I slapped the controls and the airlock door cycled. Graz zipped in first and then I stepped in, followed by the rest of the security contingent. The air smelled sour and smoky and it seemed to coat my tongue and lungs. The slightly yellow and dingy lights were flickering with the hum of ill tuned transformers cycling power through them. The walls were dirty and dingy, with what looked like burn marks on them and the floor. But for the most part, it looked almost identical to the airlocks on the Underhill, down to the controls.

That to me, just reinforced that these were from the same time period as the Underhill and the other Remnants. I looked through the window of the inner door to see people waiting about twenty yards from the doors. All looked to be wearing patchwork, archaic armor and held odd weapons. There were some well-dressed people behind them.

I noted the corridor beyond looked to be stripped to the bones, leaving only essential systems and superstructure, and scrap was stacked in piles along the walls, seemingly grouped by type. I seriously hope this wasn't representative of the condition of the rest of the Redemption.

"Graz?"

She zipped into my helmet and I closed the visor even though the indicator lights showed a breathable atmosphere on the other side of the door. I looked back to see those with SAs followed suit. After patting my shoulder to make sure the rucksack was in place, I slapped the airlock door control. The giant gears cycled, the door groaned and rotated open, like its tracks were poorly maintained.

There was a small whump when the air pressure of the two vessels equalized. That with everything else I've seen so far, worried me a little since the indicator lights showed we had equalized before I opened the door. I worried about the people here if they didn't have the resources to maintain their systems. It is good they caught up with us when they did.

I kept my arms at my side, but my hands splayed to show they were empty, though the twin MMGs on my hips and the two collapsible cold iron batons were visible.

I moved forward a few steps so that the rest of the security contingent could step aboard and I and Mother scanned the group in front of us. I noted the people I could see all had radiation burns on their skin to varying degrees, with the exception of the well-dressed people in the back.

Mother whispered in my ear, "They all seem to be suffering radiation sickness. But that is very treatable with modern medicines if it isn't lethal doses." Then before I could ask she assured me, "The radiation environment here is high, but not enough to worry about with forty-eight hours of exposure." Again, before I could ask she shared, "It is their engines. They are an old dirty fusion, small scale prototype of my World-Drives. Wasting the bulk of the fissionable materials that power them."

So by firing the engines to slow to match speed with the Leviathan, they have been poisoning themselves for decades now.

I got to business as I looked up when a man and a woman in an interesting style of white business outfits with blue jackets that had a green slash across them, stepped forward. "I'm Lieutenant Knith Shade of the Leviathan, commander of this expedition, permission to come aboard," I said.

They seemed to be scrutinizing me while their Lancers were nervously eyeing something behind me. I looked back and down to the hooves of a Minotaur then to his horns sticking out of the sides of his helmet.

Oh, Mab's tits, Knith, they've likely never seen a Minotaur before. I almost slapped my forehead, then Mother snicked up my visor so they could see me. It looked as if some of the tension and anxiety drained out of the thick, oppressive air that smelled even more sour and cloying than the airlock had.

The man said, "Oh, good, you're Human. We umm... weren't expecting any of the... others. To tell the truth, we still thought it only legend that they really existed."

I cocked my head. They hadn't expected only Humans had they? They knew we were bringing two Fae from the divided courts. I smiled crookedly, allying their apprehension. "They're just people like you and me."

I made a motion to the others, and they all dropped their visors. Besides me, there was only one other human in the security group, though heavily augmented. And I watched as all the people before us, looked from face to face, eyes blinking in shock as a half-Elf stepped to my left.

Then the two who were apparently in charge regained their wits about them and the man said, "Oh, I'm sorry, forgive us for staring, where are our manners? Permission to come aboard granted, Lieutenant. I am Captain Richter of the Redemption, and this is Captain Vandross of the Cityship Yammato. We are pleased to make your acquaintance on this auspicious occasion. The meeting of peoples long separated."

I took a couple of steps forward and offered my hand, the nano-plates of my gauntlets melting back as I did so. His eyes widened at the tech, then shook my hand with the grip of someone who grew up in this lighter gravity, but it would still be respectable in a D-Ring.

I noted the skin on his wrist showed radiation burn lesions. Captain Vandross shook my hand heartily and said in a rich alto voice with a different accent than Richter, "It is nice to put a face to the voice."

I nodded. "With the radiation interference, audio was the best we could do. But with the Quantum Entanglement gear we brought, you'll have real-time audio, video, and data streams from the Leviathan. And I'm happy to put a face to the voices too."

Then I said, "And let me introduce you to the representative of the lesser Fae here, Graz, Sprite of Beta-Stack-C."

Graz zipped out of my helmet squeaking out as she held a tiny hand out to them, "Pleased to meet ya." They stumbled back in shock and a few Lancers started to raise their weapons. Richter caught himself then held a hand out low and the weapons were lowered as the man and woman studied Graz intently.

"What? You don't speak English? What about Ship Common? Celtic? Chinese? Russian?" She was cycling through languages even I didn't know with perfect accents. She looked at me. "Are these Bigs broken or something?"

I muttered, "Graz!"

Then Richter held a hand out and said, "I apologize, we've just never seen a real Fairy before."

"Fairy?! Did you just call me a..." I grabbed her moth wings and pulled her in front of my face, then made a zipping motion over her lips. She exhaled, crossed her arms over her chest obstinately then she hovered in a pout when I released her.

I turned to the Captains. "I'm sorry, but she's a Sprite, she very touchy about Fairies."

He nodded as he eyed my Sprite. "Of course, my apologies... Graz."

Then offered a hand again and Graz grudgingly shook his finger, the repeated the greeting when Vandross did the same.

Then I said as I turned back, "Let me introduce you to your counterpart, Secretary Y'nell of the State Department and the rest of our delegation."

Y'nell stepped out of the airlock as regal as a royal. I almost sighed in resignation, all the political posturing was about to begin. And I, unfortunately, was going to have a front-row seat since I was responsible for guarding him and the others until we departed. Fun. Just fuck me now and space me naked.

I got nervous when the Greater Fae stepped out behind him. Every Lancer had instinctively raised their weapons halfway, and everyone was silent for four long heartbeats before Y'nell took the reins and said, "Shall we retire to more suitable surroundings to do proper introductions and talk? And leave the workers to unload the supplies and our relief workers can start medical assessment of those you indicated were most in need?"

Richter nodded. "Of course. This way please."

I whispered in my helmet, "Well that went smoothly."

"Not."

"Oh shush, Mother."

We moved with two of us in front with the secretary and the rest of our unit flanking our group and taking up the rear, leaving two guards at the airlock. Some Lancers to the front and rear.

The Captain said to Secretary Y'nell, "Our people will arrive at the Underhill soon to help unload the supplies you brought and to escort your relief crew around the ring, Mr. Secretary."

As Y'nell responded, Myra was contacting me directly on the Brigade channel, "Um, Knith, we have movement out here, some smaller vessels are moving this way from that asteroid tethered to the other Cityship. I think I might just go watch things from the cockpit of my fighter for a bit."

Mother responded in my voice with a thought from me, "Oh, hang tight Kitty Cat, let me look into it. Likely just some lookie-loos."

"Kitty Cat?"

"What? That's what you always called her back in college. I have all your com records here."

"Yeah, when I was dating her. Just space me now. And stop digging into my com records."

She huffed.

I glanced around as we moved through the corridor, I asked as my eyes scanned everything for Mother to record, "Captain, there seem to be some smaller ships heading this way from the Yammato."

Richter turned and looked at me, then my armor and helmet. "Those would be mining ships. Either they are delivering ore to the refinery or their curiosity has gotten the better of them." Then he nudged his chin at me. "We haven't seen gear anything like your party is equipped with before."

Shrugging I said, "Engineers and magi-tech practitioners on the Worldship continue to innovate."

Captain Vandross asked excitedly, "So you still have resources on the Leviathan? Magi-tech? What does that mean? Is your gear... magic?"

I glanced around at the corridor that looked stripped bare of anything not vital. Didn't they engineer these vessels with enough resources to make the interstellar journey? I nodded again and said absently, "Some of the systems are a melding of magic and technology. My Scatter Armor, for example, blunts and dissipates magical attacks to a degree."

The captains exchanged looks and I realized that unless there were any new practicing witches on old Earth, magic was likely just an abstract concept to them instead of a day to day reality.

The Secretary shot me an annoyed look. Right, I'm there to be seen, not heard. I just inclined my head to them then shut my mouth. Mother selected a song from the anthropological archives to play in my head, 'Heart and Soul' by a band called T'Pau. Were they Elvish?

We stepped through a manually operated door with a large wheel to seal it airtight and into a large open space that felt more natural to me as it curved up into the horizon on both sides, though oddly, there were no Day Lights, only girders and bulkhead a couple of hundred yards above.

There was a wide road-like corridor between ramshackle structures that seemed stacked upon each other. It was like a metal village, with people everywhere in what looked like some sort of shops and marketplace in the road facing shops. I'd say a farmer's market, but everyone seemed to be selling wares made from scrap, and no food was to be seen in any of the booths.

Everything was dirty, rusty, and smelling of the thick oppressive atmosphere. I think I even smelled human waste mixed in. It was like the slums of the C and D rings back home. All the people wore tattered clothes and had radiation burns and lesions on their skin. They shied away from the Lancers and the Captains, but as soon as they passed, our group was mobbed by people showing off their wares. Some saw most of us were not human and actually screamed and ran in a panic. But most were fascinated and more interested in trying to get us to purchase their trinkets than fleeing.

I wondered absently what they used for money here. Was it a chit based monetary system like we used? It looked more likely that they used a barter system by what I was witnessing.

Then my breath hitched, seeing in the mix, children with the same radiation burns on their faces and arms. I grabbed my rucksack off my shoulders. A Lancer moved closer, lifting his weapon slightly as I unzipped the bag and started pulling candies, cakes, granola bars, jerky, and some toys that Graz' family had gathered up for me, and started pressing them into the hands of the children. Some grabbed at what I gave others but once a child had something from me, they held onto it with ferocity as they dashed away into the maze of structures.

Someone shouted, "Food!" And the place exploded into chaos. The crowds surged forward, pressing in on us, all caution over the non-humans with us forgotten as men, women, and children all started shouting about food and putting their hands out, grabbing at us.

The music cut out as I said over our tac channel, "Everyone. Give them whatever food you have. Rations, candy, jerky, gum..." Our people were handing out what little they had tucked into their gear as I was showing everyone my rucksack was now empty, and they kept pushing in on us until my ears started ringing at some loud banging sounds, and I saw sparks on the bulkhead above.

People screamed and ran and I looked around as I drew my twin MMGs, just to see some of the Lancers had their weapons pointed up, their barrels were smoking. Were those... were those projectile weapons? In space? On a spaceship? Were they insane?

It was as if the place had magically become deserted. Even carts and wagons were left behind as the people all scattered and disappeared into the buildings and shacks of metal. I saw people looking thorough metal shutters at us just standing in the middle of the deserted ring. Then Richter muttered, "Scavengers and savages." Then he put on a politician's smile and said, "Sorry about that. The workers get testy around protein dispersal."

As we started moving again, Y'nell asked the question on all our minds as we watched the eyes watching us, "Protein dispersal?"

Vandross shared, "Of course, the daily dispersal of protein and water rations for each person. You do the same I assume on the Leviathan?"

The Secretary said distractedly as he looked at the dilapidated structures we passed, "Do you not have agriculture and livestock to feed your people? Of course, we have monthly meal card vouchers you can use at the dispensaries or any participating restaurants or grocery stores."

They looked confused over most of what he said, but Richter supplied, "We have the algae vats and soybean hydroponics. Reprocessed water. They supply all the nutritional needs of the Cityships. Leaders and the Lancers have some of the fruit and vegetable crops from what is left of the old agricultural domes, but those are for the elite."

Algae and soy? That was all these people ate? And it was rationed?

I heard myself asking, "Has it always been like this?" as I realized we were standing on what was essentially a ghost ship. Sure, there were twenty-five thousand souls on each Cityship, but this wasn't living, was it? Our prisoners mining the Heart had more than the people here.

Vandross shared, "The historical data files that we have pieced together show it was different in the beginning. The six stations that supported the building of the great Worldship were retrofitted and launched to save more of the human race, to travel to that new planet which only their descendants would see one day."

Richter continued for her, "But as ship systems failed, or vessels were damaged beyond repair, ships compliments would be moved to the other ships, and the abandoned vessel stripped for resources. Blight killed off much of the crops in the domes just as sicknesses swept thorough out populations, killing large numbers. But we persevered. The last two of the Cityships have finally reached the Leviathan at long last. Our promised home is within our grasp finally."

There had been six Cityships, and only these two had survived? We were only halfway to our destination and looking at the current condition of the vessels and crew, they wouldn't make it more than a couple more generations. It was good they were able to catch up with us. Maybe together we could find a solution to their generations of problems here.

Chapter 7 – The Whole of the Moon

The control center was a counterpoint to the conditions we saw in the quarter-mile walk. It was clean and almost sterile, white walls everywhere, though there was evidence of centuries of jury-rigging of systems. And some equipment looked out of place, though clean and white like everything else.

The Lancers lined up against one wall as the Captains led us up to a raised platform in the middle of the space, where dozens of people dressed in white with those blue jackets with that green slash, were manning stations all around with hundreds of screens surrounding them.

They all looked up as we stepped up onto the platform. My eyes were flicking around the screens. A couple had data streaming, and a communications station had transmit logs with the Leviathan labeled on it. Then the majority of the screens were displays from internal and external cameras. Half were labeled Redemption and the other half Yammato. There were three exterior views on each, with one viewing each Cityship.

The rest were all monitoring all the occupied spaces of the ships. The people who were just barely surviving.

I saw I wasn't the only one from our expedition noticing all of this. Especially the fact that two lower screens displayed the Greater Fae from our group. I looked at the angle, then from Delphine to where the source of the signal would be, and saw cameras on the shoulders of a couple of the Lancers. These people were very serious about security.

I was tuning out as the Captain gave a brief introduction of his senior staff to our diplomats, as he spoke of the cutting edge technology integrated into their Central Control. But he had my attention when he said to one of the workers, "Raise the blast doors please Emmett?"

The other man nodded and hit a control. The far wall thrummed and seemed to split horizontally, as two massive bulkhead doors opened behind what looked to be a window that was at least three meters thick. We were treated to the familiar view of the nebula we were flying past and the brilliant star-field beyond as it rotated past, then the Yammato filled the view and rotated past.

These Cityships really were pretty spectacular. Not as awe-inspiring as our Worldship mind you, but still amazing feats of engineering to still be flying after all these years.

When I turned back to the room, I noted that all eyes were on our group. Well, most of our group except for me and the other Human. I was used to that, being ignored as a Human, but these were other Humans, and the looks on their faces weren't those of curiosity looking at the other races, it was something I couldn't quite place my finger on.

Captain Vandross addressed Secretary Y'nell. "Mr. Secretary, our arbiters... diplomats, are eager to speak with your people. Please join us in the planning room?" She indicated one of the doors along the back wall.

I started moving with them when he responded with a perfectly... diplomatic, "Of course." But stopped and looked down to the hand on my chest. I looked up to Captain Richter, and he gave me a smile that didn't reach his eyes. "Lieutenant, this is the most secure section of the ship. Outliers cannot access it. Your people are safe, our Lancers will be out here to assure we are not disturbed."

Before I could argue, Y'nell said, "Lieutenant... please return to the ship with your contingent and help coordinate the transfer of supplies with Cityship personnel. This initial session will take most of the day. Return for us at nineteen hundred hours ship-time."

I shook my head and said through my teeth as I gave a forced smile, "I can't do that. My orders are..."

"Changed." He had a smarmy smirk as he showed his wrist console to me. "The President agrees with me that a military presence is not necessary when in discussions of aid and medical relief. Counterproductive if you will."

Blinking and not believing what I was hearing, I said, "Mother, connect me with President Yang please." He'd been communicating with Yang while we were being escorted here?

The President must have been waiting for my call because she responded almost instantly without greeting, "Shade. Statesmanship is a delicate process, something at odds with your particular flavor of doing things. Please stand down until Secretary Y'nell calls for you? The parameters of your mission have changed."

"Well hello to you too, Madame President."

"Don't get flippant, Lieutenant."

"Sorry, ma'am."

And the channel was cut from her end. It was all I could do to stop spitting out every curse word I knew. This new course of action was ill-advised and just threw operational security out the door. I just looked at the smug Elvish face that was staring at me and said through gritted teeth as I inclined my head in capitulation, "Mr. Secretary. Nineteen hundred hours ship-time."

I motioned for the security detail to return to the airlock. They were all looking at me, even more dumbfounded than I was. How could these damn politicians be so idiotic? My people started to file out, with some Lancers flanking them.

Richter was staring at me, eyes wide. "You were speaking directly with the Leviathan?" I nodded and he asked in wonder, "That's the quantum entanglement communication system you're sharing with us?" I nodded again.

I think the smile he was now beaming our way was the first genuine one I have seen on this vessel. Then he turned from me and made an ushering motion to our oblivious politicians. "Ladies and gentlemen?"

They started to follow, and when a wary looking Delphine passed by I grabbed her wrist and she turned to look in my eyes, not looking down at my wrist console I had just latched to her. The Fae virtually never used wrist consoles. She just inclined her head and followed the others as I snicked up my visor and said to Mother without activating my external speakers, "Monitor and log everything that goes on in there. If you suspect anything hinky, let me know."

She said in a very serious tone, "Of course Knith." I nodded to myself. At least Delphine and her Summer Court counterpart seemed as uncomfortable with the situation as me. She never would have accepted my wrist console otherwise.

Then I turned and followed the rest of my unit out of the Control Center. Two Lancers on my heels as I reviewed in my head, everything I have seen on the Cityship so far... literally as Mother had anticipated me and was replaying everything from my helmet-cams since we entered the airlock in my peripheral vision. I assured her, "You're a wonder lady."

"I know."

"And modest too."

"Aren't I just?"

Then I asked out of curiosity, "Does this place..."

"Creep me the fuck out, to use your vernacular?"

I tried not to chuckle and said, "Yeah, that."

"Yes."

Then I asked as I turned my head in my helmet a little, "What about you Graz?"

I was met with silence. "Graz? Mab preserve us all, where'd the flying pain in my ass get off to now? She shouldn't be wandering around a foreign spaceship."

Mother responded, "She shut off her micro-wrist console so I cannot track her telemetry. She had shut it off when the people in the market mobbed you."

That shows just how damn distracted I had been to not notice she hadn't been with me the whole time. Now I was worried shitless. I had to remind myself that the Sprite has survived for thousands of years without me, so I was sure she was fine.

When we passed back through the market, I noted the people were all going about their business, eyes down, not crowding us or offering their wares like the last time. When one man started to look up at us as he grabbed some trinkets from his table, he looked back down and backed away when a man in the crowd, dressed in tatters like the others, but with a blue and green armband tied to his arm took a step toward him. The vendor looked positively cowed.

I glanced around and saw others with the same armband sprinkled throughout the crowd. Were these the Outliers that were causing problems on the Cityships? Were they a... gang?

We didn't have many gang problems on the World. Whenever they popped up, the Enforcers would bring the law down on their asses. It is amazing how many questionable life choices can be rectified with a little hard time in the mines in the Heart.

A little boy, maybe five or six, with one milky eye near a radiation burn on his cheek ran up to me before anyone could stop him. He was holding up a scrap of metal that was twisted to look like a bird. I crouched as I lowered my visor, then shot a death glare at a woman with an armband who was moving our way. She froze and I squatted in front of the boy.

He smiled at me and touched my helmet in awe. I looked at the little bird he seemed to be offering me. I smiled widely at him. "I'm sorry, I don't know what you use for money here. I have this..." I reached into a belt pouch and pulled out a small emergency button light. I tapped it and it lit up then tapped it again and it shut off. I pinned it to his tattered shirt and accepted the little bird.

He was grinning widely as he started turning the little light off and on, then he just dashed back into the crowd to join a woman who wrapped an arm around his shoulders. I placed his trinket carefully into my pack and stood. I looked at my shadows. "Come along then." They didn't say a word, just fell in behind me as I rushed to catch up with the rest of the security detachment.

I admit, I breathed a sigh of relief the moment we set foot back on the Underhill, leaving the Lancers outside the airlock. That lasted a moment as all my people started blurting out, "What the fuck, Shade?" "Were we really dismissed?" "What kind of idiots send away their protection on a foreign ship?"

I held a hand up. "The little weasel has been talking with President Yang. So right now, we follow orders."

A Dwarf growled out, "And if things go FUBAR, we take the blame. Right?"

I chuckled. "Just as all other things politic go."

They all chuckled nervously with me.

Mac came up the corridor, brow creased and eyes pinched. "Where's the rest?"

Shaking my head I said, "Doing what diplomats do."

"Fucking up the world?"

"Pretty much." I pressed the little metal bird into his hand. "Your souvenir."

He squinted at it and prompted, "What is it."

I sighed and gave him a sad smile and told him the truth, "About the most precious, heartfelt, and priceless thing on that ship. Don't lose it."

He looked at it with new eyes, and it was as if he could see the value I saw in it and the boy who had held it before me. Then he nodded and walked beside me with it balanced on his hand as if it were made of spun silver. I called to our people. "Take five then get with the Underhill Quartermaster about aiding in the transfer of supplies."

One called back to me, "Where are you going?"

I shrugged. "The mess."

Then I told Mac, "I need to empty your galley of everything but what we'll need for the return trip."

"And why would I let you do that?"

I looked at him and said plainly, "I'll pay for it all somehow if the President doesn't comp you for it. People are starving on this ship... children."

Without another word, not even his infuriating habit of bartering an unfair price from me, he just led the way to the galley with purposeful strides. Sometimes I just loved the man.

Music started playing over the intercom as we started pulling all the foodstuffs out of storage and started loading crates. Mother identified the music as the 'Whole of the Moon', by the Waterboys.

Chapter 8 – We Are the World

The rest of the day was spent helping the quartermaster coordinate supplies and sending security details out with the relief workers as they were led around to evaluate the citizens of the Redemption most in need of medical assistance.

Our doctors tell me that the medical services and personnel on the ships are woefully ill-equipped to handle all but the most basic of medical emergencies, and they apparently have no treatment available to mitigate radiation poisoning, which is virtually never fatal on the World as it is very treatable and reversible with time. Such treatments are critical on spacecraft traveling through high cosmic radiation expanses of interstellar space.

I was reviewing the data and visuals from Myra after I secured clearance for her to fly around the twin vessels to evaluate them for damage and space-worthiness.

One thing struck me as strange, and it had her as well since she had highlighted the damage around the section of the Yammato which had been torn away. The burns and melted metal at the shear zone looked to be burns made by high energy weapons instead of space debris.

We postulated, "Perhaps they used their mining ships to shear off some dangerous debris after the damage had occurred?"

When we were silent for a bit as I just stared at the data, she asked, "That's it? You aren't going to contact them to inquire?"

I smirked and asked as I switched over to the data feed from my wrist console on Delphine's arm, "I notice that you didn't either."

She chuckled and purred out, "I'm glad to see things aren't adding up for you either. I thought it was just me."

Shaking my head I said, "Even Mother has an uneasy feeling about this whole thing."

"It..."

I repeated Mother's words to her, "Creeps you the fuck out?"

"Precisely."

While I read over the dialogue of the diplomatic meeting, I absently shunted a feed from my helmet to her so she could see the reactions of the people in the ring and their condition. She was silent for a long time as she slowly flew back to dock with the Underhill.

I prompted since she technically held a higher rank than me even though I was the commander of the mission, "You hold the fort here? Mac and I have something we need to do." The schematics of the interior of the Cityships were pulled up in my peripheral, courtesy of the detailed scans of the ships from Myra's magi-tech enhanced sensor sweeps.

"Rodger dodger, Fae-lips."

Fae-lips? Just space me now, I hope nobody on the secondary tac-frequency was listening, I'd die of embarrassment if that got around. "Shut your feline face."

She chuckled as I went back to the scans.

We had only seen about one percent of the inner ring volume. And the scattered returns showed that the ramshackle dwellings and business district was pretty much strung out along three quarters the circumference of the Redemption.

I sighed when I looked over at the two mag-loader sleds piled with foodstuffs, knowing we wouldn't even make a dent, but at least maybe some families wouldn't go hungry for one night. What I was doing hadn't been sanctioned by either side, so I looked around for someone who would step up to help me with the second sled, but blinked when I saw Mac holding the controls for it with Mir... in clothes... beside him.

I asked, "You sure? I mean... you're the Underhill's master."

The man shrugged as he started the sled moving. "Jane's at the helm."

Ah.

When half the security unit that wasn't already escorting our people started to move out with us I held up a stopping hand. "This is off the books, people. We'll be fine. Commander Udriel is in charge while I'm out. Jane Doe is in command of the ship."

They all looked put out, they knew what we were doing and wanted to come, but if I was going to see a reprimand for this, I didn't want to drag anyone else down with me. Mac and Mir, not being citizens of the Leviathan, could do whatever they wanted without repercussions... within reason.

To my surprise, one of the few Orcish women on the world stepped up and handed me a couple items of food. "From my personal stash." I looked up to the six-foot ten woman and nodded my thanks, then was surprised when a couple others did the same.

Just as we reached the airlock I stopped dead, Madame Zoe was standing there, wrinkled and withered, her glassy eyes looking through me as she said, "Know the enemy within us, Knith Shade, or the journey ends in the middle before it even starts."

Clairvoyants freaked me out in more ways than one. Humans who embraced witchery burned their own physical and mental energy in exchange for a sliver of the power the Fae threw around lazily every day with no ill effects. This is why all the stories of witches and all their derivatives in human history conjure up the very image of Madame Zoe in our heads. Withered and wrinkled, looking at the ends of their lives at just thirty or forty.

I don't care if that power brings them the wisdom of people many times their age, why would you trade your life away like that? And the clairvoyants and oracles were even more frightening, because they spoke in riddles, since their minds were warped by the magics, and it was hard to tell if their words were truly prophetic or if they were just the ramblings of a broken mind. I always viewed them as unwitting charlatans, but Madam Zoe has always been too close for comfort with her riddles than I cared to admit.

Then she smiled her almost toothless smile and held something up to me. "Butterscotch?"

Mac stepped up to her and cupped his hands around hers. "Not now dear. Young Shade and I are needed elsewhere."

He looked up and one of his crew-members, whom I didn't know, hustled up and took her arm gently. She smiled at the Satyr and offered, "Butterscotch?" The man inclined his head and smiled at the woman as he led her away. She hesitated only a moment and called back, "The father is exposed." Then she started singing to herself as she was led away.

Mac nodded as if heeding wise words then looked at me. "Lead on, child."

Mir virtually draped herself on me as we moved out. I spoke out of the side of my mouth to her, "Nice outfit."

She smiled and said, "Thanks. I got it from your quarters."

Son of a... I rolled my eyes at her. I wasn't going to complain since the last thing these people needed to see was a naked mirror skinned woman parading around on their world. Then I exhaled when she asked, her brow furrowed, "Where's Graz? I haven't seen her all day."

I sighed. "Doing what Graz does."

"Spying, or getting into trouble?" Mir asked.

"Likely both."

The moment we exited the airlock onto the Redemption, my shadows stood from where they were sitting on the stacks of scavenged materials in the corridor. I prompted before they could speak, "Where's the most heavily populated area within walking distance?"

One started to say as he pointed the opposite way we had gone before, "Little Manila is just..." The other one backhanded him hard and glared at him. The other man just shut up.

I just started moving and the senior man said, "I don't have records of any more supplies. Manifest?"

Mac said before I could, "I'm the master of the Underhill here, I've got foodstuffs to trade at your markets while these do-gooders play politics. Profit is profit, and I'm not making any just sitting on my ass attached to your airlock."

The man exchanged a knowing look with Mac then said, "Of course we'll have to inspect for contraband."

Mac nodded and stepped back. I looked at him and he nudged his eyes so I stepped back too. The men looked in the first couple containers, and the senior man took a box of crackers and a box of juices and said, "Our fee for permitting you to trade on the Cityships."

Mac was very accommodating, and I've seen the man almost go into apoplexy when Graz cheated him out of a single chit on a half-burned thermo-coupling. Instead of getting upset, he just smiled widely and inclined his head. "Of course."

Then the man motioned us past and we moved out of the corridor and into the ring envelope. I turned the way to where the other man had pointed and started walking with our Lancer shadows at our backs.

We didn't go far before the density of people and makeshift structures were five or six times heavier than the first barter market we had visited. It was counter-intuitive that there would be fewer people closer to the control center for the ship.

Mother sensed my apprehension at what I was seeing and started playing a haunting tune, 'We Are the World', by a variety of artists that scrolled in my vision for quite some time.

For the longest time, people just moved aside to let us pass, all eyes were on Mir. I glanced at her and had to double-take. She loved being the center of attention normally, but this was the first time I had seen her nervous as she just looked around at all the people watching her, eyes darting.

Then Mac stopped, and I brought my sled to a halt next to him. We exchanged a look and then started opening crates as I called out, "We've food from the Worldship to share." I held out a package of cookies toward a woman who had a cart full of what looked like twisted wire necklaces on display. "Please everyone, just take one item and let others get some."

The woman looked at me, eyes wide, then she looked over her shoulder and I followed her gaze, a woman with one of those armbands was standing on the second level just above the marketplace looking down at us. When the watcher didn't say or do anything, the woman almost dove on my offering.

As soon as she had it, she handed it down to a little girl who looked like her, and the girl crawled through a loose vent on the side of the first structure as many hands tried to grab the prize from her hands.

Then all hells broke loose again as the crowds surged toward us, murmurs of "food," filtering all around us as Mir, Mac, and I tried to keep people from grabbing right out of the containers as we handed items out.

When it was getting a little rough, people screamed and started running when the Lancers again fired off their weapons into the air, the projectiles sparking and ricocheting off of the structure above. The senior man roared out, "Settle down you filthy animals! You heard them, just one item and move on! Form lines!"

And the people scrambled to do what the rudely brash man had ordered. The lines formed almost too quickly. I realized this was probably what they had to do when the protein rations were dispensed once a day here.

Mir and I exchanged looks, then we started handing things out in an orderly fashion as people waited their turn. I had never seen so many desperate people in my life. When I glanced over at Mac, he looked stricken, especially when a child stepped up.

People were thanking us, and a few insisted we take something in exchange. They left us with all sorts of handmade wares. All looked to be made from scavenged scraps. One woman with a child hugged me. And before I released her I whispered, "Who are the people with the armbands?" I had noted six or seven hanging around, but none of them got in line.

She whispered back, her voice wavering in fear as she started to shake, "Outliers." I nodded thanks. Then reached into the last bin for the next person just to come up empty-handed. I rummaged through the other containers then looked to Mir and Mac and they shook their heads. There were still so many people in line.

I called out, "We're sorry, that's all the supplies we have left on our ship. If we return, we'll bring more."

It was almost as if a wave of depression, disappointment, and even despair rolled through those in line. Then the people started moving away, except for a few who moved around Mir. Asking questions, reaching out to touch her. Some were asking if she were Fae or even a robot. She informed them, "I assure you, I'm human, like you. I just have a lot of augments."

I noted a young woman who was barely older than a teen, her pretty face and arms marred by a rash and radiation burns, as she squatted by the containers on the sled. She reached out and tapped one with the tip of a finger listening like she was trying to determine what they were made of.

I looked at her, crouched and smiled, then asked, "Do you want one? Take it. It can be useful to store things or I'm sure you can use it for materials to create other things." Without a word, she beamed a huge smile at me, and grabbed one and ran off through the crowd, like she were afraid I'd change my mind.

Others saw this and some started to line up again. I told my companions, "Give them the containers and crates." And so it went. And when there was nothing else but the gifts the others had heaped on us, we bid our farewells, promising that if we were allowed another visit, that we'd bring more when we returned.

I sighed as I looked around, then started back to the Underhill. I felt so... emotionally drained. It was like my soul was just dragging behind me as we went. Mir looked stupefied, and Mac... Mac looked mad. Not just mad, but like he was using all his willpower not to simply blow up and combust on the spot.

He reminded us, "That could so easily be the Leviathan." It made me to aware of how delicate a balance our world truly was in. With the wrong combination of catastrophes, we would be living that way too. In an instance like that, the immortal beings on our ship would likely be the only ones to arrive at the new world with a virtual ghost ship if that occurred.

I just sat in the cockpit with Mac, Mir, Jane, and Myra and contemplated how emptying an entire ship's stores hadn't put a dent in the overwhelming need for... well for everything on these ancient flying wrecks.

When a chime went off, signaling it time for me to go escort our people home, I was grateful to have a task to keep my mind off the dark spiral I was in.

Chapter 9 – Smoke On the Water

The next day was worse, besides escorting the medical and relief staff around while the politicians did their diplomatic thing, there was nothing to do except sit on the Underhill and try not to think about the people out there.

I sat on the bridge, looking at some of the cleverly fashioned trinkets we were gifted by the residents. One I especially liked. It was some sort of round piece of metal that looked to have been some sort of access cover at one point, it had been hammered flat and drawn on with what looked like charcoal.

The artist had been incredible, depicting a scene with what I was assuming was their interpretation of the inhabitants of Fairie in an alien-looking forest, pointing to six stars in a row in the sky. I touched the stars with my fingertips. Myra sat up from where she was filling out status reports to file with Mother. "What's that?"

I showed it to her and her cat ear implants twitched as her eyes widened, "That's stunning."

As I nodded, I pointed at the stars. "I think it is depicting Planetfall. These stars being the six Cityships that began their journey, and these must be the Fae from the Leviathan looking up to see the new arrivals."

"They don't look anything like the Fae."

Shrugging I supplied, "No, but their people have never seen a Fae. And from what I saw, they don't have their original computer core as most of the systems were manually switched by people manning all the stations. No AI to do it for them. So they likely don't have any visual records of the varied races that joined the Humans on the Worldship either."

Mir said from over my shoulder, "Beautiful, I've never seen such fine artwork done with such primitive tools before."

Mac just mumbled something from the Captain's chair. I narrowed my eyes. He was there before I turned in, and he was there when I woke to get in some exercise before escorting our diplomats back to continue their discussions, and he was still there, looking through terabytes of information Mother was supplying him.

Mir followed my gaze, then said as she strode over to him to place her hands on her hips, "He hasn't moved from there since we returned yesterday." Then she said louder, enunciating each syllable, "He needs to get some sleep or he'll be useless when we undock tonight."

He didn't even look up, he just absently waved her off, growling gruffly, "Sleep is for the young or the dead. I'm neither."

I opened my mouth but Mir just huffed out a breath she didn't need. "Don't bother, he's too obstinate to listen."

I prompted for about the tenth time, "What is so important about the files you are sifting through?"

He finally looked up and told me like it were obvious, "Historical records from the construction of the Leviathan. Knowledge is power. I'm arming myself."

I looked at the data stream being fed to him in the lower right of my field of view and exhaled. He was consuming almost a gigabyte a minute. Did he think I wouldn't notice? His game of pretending to be someone else was crumbling slowly around him no matter how much he denied it.

I thought to Mother, "Is he skimming the data or reading it?"

She responded, almost carefully, "He is accessing every byte of data, but only as fast as the old systems on the Underhill can receive them. I suspect he can assimilate data as fast as some of my subsystems."

Then I glanced at the door when the quartermaster stepped in. I almost blurted, "Any word?"

He shook his head. "No contact with Graz yet."

I prompted, "Mother?"

She answered mechanically, "No mention of her on any of the Cityship communication channels."

Frustration had me pacing the cockpit deck again. I had found her tiny wrist console tucked between my armor and my skinsuit when I asked Mother to ping it. That was both promising and worrying.

She knew what she was doing when she went out snooping. If we could track her wrist console, maybe the Redemption could trace its emissions too. But it also meant that she couldn't contact us if she ran into trouble.

She knew our departure time, so I held out hope she'd be here in time. We couldn't hold launch to wait for her without Richter knowing she was on their vessel. If she didn't make it back, she'd have to fend for herself until the next diplomatic visit or when they caught up with the Leviathan in a little over a month.

I tried not to dwell on the fact that she wasn't with us by going over our medical staff's health evaluations of the residents of these floating death traps. It looked grim. With the exception of a few dire cases, there were thousands in need of medical intervention mostly because of tissue and organ damage from the radiation their engines were spewing.

Our people ran out of meds to treat the radiation sickness in some people with severe cases in just an hour yesterday. Now they were coordinating with Med-Tech back on the world, trying to come up with a solution to treat the people most in need faster than it would take to fly another mission out.

The prevailing plan was to wait just a few days until they were in the range of one of the massive tugs to act as sort of a medical triage carrier, and now that the Underhill's cargo bay was empty, we would be bringing as many high-risk patients back with us as we could. We secured sixty cots there with mag-anchors for the trip. We had water enough though food would be scarce, but it would be only a couple days as the distance was diminishing by the hour.

Madame Zoe, surprisingly, could help there. It seems the clairvoyant has quite the green thumb and has a mini hydroponics garden set up in a maintenance storeroom next to her cabin. I guess it has been passed down for generations in her clan aboard the Underhill since Exodus.

It not only provided her clan and the ship with a small amount of food during tough times but also provided a small amount of oxygen and CO_2 filtering for the vessel as well to aid the environmental processing systems. The more I learned about the secrets the Underhill and her crew, the more impressed I got.

I noted when I reviewed the footage of the diplomatic feeds that Delphine was transmitting to us, that the Captains and their council members, all wearing those same blue jackets with green slashes, seemed to have quite a lot of fresh food available, even in excess as porters brought in meals for everyone in the conference room a couple times a day.

For the Leviathan, it was just modest fare, though with no meats, but for here? It was virtually a banquet while people were literally starving in the streets. I had to contemplate that for a while, wondering how it was any different than us. We still had homeless who only ate what they could afford with the monthly meal cards, while our leaders and rich ate like royalty. We just happened to have more available to us, so our destitute still didn't starve.

Would our elite give up their luxury if our people suffered the same calamities as the Cityships? Or would they sacrifice for the people? I didn't know the answer to that, I could only hope they would do... better since it wasn't sitting well with me here after seeing the desperation of the people here.

When it was time for us to return to the control center to escort our delegates back to the Underhill, I took the time to eavesdrop a little as the Lancers and the technicians spoke in low tones away from us. My hearing and sight are better than the average Human's and I've taken advantage of that fact in situations like this. Half the races on board had better hearing, so I was sure some of the others in our group were hearing the same thing.

The Lancers were asking someone at a security console, "How can you stand to be so close to the 'roaches'?" The reply was just as perplexing. "It's just for a little while longer. Our birthright is near."

I had a feeling they weren't talking about insects.

When our people joined us, the Secretary was looking quite pleased with himself as were most of the group, but the two Greater Fae had inscrutable expressions on their faces as they studied the two Captains who were graciously thanking our people. Delphine didn't pull her eyes away as she absently pressed my wrist console into my hand.

Richter was saying, "We'll send word to load the patients along with what little water we can spare onto the Stingers. Our people will bring the worst cases to the Underhill. I look forward to meeting with this President Yang, face to face after how kind your people have been to us. This is an exciting time to live in."

I whispered, "What's that all about?"

Delphine finally looked away from them and just nudged her chin toward Y'nell, who was making a beeline toward me as she whispered, "The gift that keeps on giving." Then she gave the man a smile that was an insult to all other fake smiles which came before it.

It was lost on the man as he puffed up like a glow-frog and said like it was the best news in the world. "Captain Richter will be joining us on the trip back, so he can speak with the President and the Queens himself."

That actually was pretty interesting, but then my eyes narrowed as four armored and heavily armed Lancers moved up behind the Captain. "We're not letting any armed people on the Underhill. Operational safety is my job."

He shook his head. "Relax, it is a gesture of goodwill between our peoples, just like he let you and your armed team escort us on their ship. Besides, I've cleared it with President Yang. You should be getting confirmation at any moment."

True to his word, I got a presidential communique pinging in my heads up and Mother started it scrolling as she muttered in my head, "Blah blah blah... escort the leader of the Cityships... blah blah blah... convoy of ships... blah blah blah..."

I chuckled and assured her, "Three ships do not a convoy make."

It was as if I could hear her shaking her head as a section of the long-winded change of orders highlighted and was brought forward to fill my vision. "She authorized this? Did she run this by the Brigade higher-ups? Surely they wouldn't have authorized this on a moment's notice."

Mother sighed and I asked the Secretary, "Seriously? We're escorting seventy ships full of patients back to the Leviathan?"

That was what the talk of Stingers was. Those mining ships. They were going to send them with sick citizens into interstellar space between here and the Worldship? They were little more than flying relics themselves, all patched together over the centuries. And the orders expected us to launch on schedule. We wouldn't have time to inspect that many ships, or even a handful of them at that time since we were to launch in two hours.

Mother fairy humper!

Then I sighed and asked Richter who had just joined us, "What is the compliment of each Stinger?"

He said, "Usually two. The pilot and the stinger-tech... the mining specialist who operates the mining laser and the capture arms. But we'll be forgoing the specialist so two patients can be transported by the pilots."

I mentally added two hundred and ten to the sixty we would be ferrying in the Underhill, plus Richter and four Lancers. One hundred and seventy-five Cityshippers. Space me now. And it sounded as if they were only going to have water in the other ships, no food for two days.

Would just a few more days make that much of a difference? I thought of the women and children with lesions all over their skin and sighed. Every minute of suffering we could alleviate was worth the disarray this threw in our own operations.

I had to ask, "Our pilots have seen your Stingers. They look rough, will they be able to make the flight safely?"

He assured us, "They are built like tanks. They can survive a direct meteoroid strike and keep on mining. Their engines are oversize to push around the ore they free from the asteroid, so they will be able to make the crossing. It will utilize most of the reaction fuel they have left, but I am assured by your government that some could be freed up from the Leviathan stores to replenish what is used since it is a humanitarian mission."

I felt ashamed that I felt it wasn't a good idea again, that we'd be dipping into the reserves to fuel so many ships when just by waiting a few days, we could save that fuel for when the Leviathan really needed it. Our own asteroid in the Heart was being depleted of resources faster than the designers had anticipated, this would just put a further strain on things.

But smarter people than me had to have already calculated this and determined we could part with that much fuel. Otherwise, they would have never agreed to this. So this had to be the best way we could help as many people as we could in the most expeditious way.

I inclined my head to the man and he said, "Then we should make haste if we're to help load the patients onto the Underhill. I have to say I am quite curious about it. The AJAX-43 appears in hundreds of texts from the construction records of the Worldship. It sounds quite improbable and incredible at the same time. Especially for an Ore Runner built around the same time as the shipyard stations, our

Cityships were built from. Our external cameras show it to be in almost pristine condition still."

They knew about the Underhill?

A minute later we were heading back to our ship, my eyes scanning the crowds for the Outliers. They were usually easy to spot with their armbands, but I couldn't see any. I was also frantically scanning the area for the telltale dust from Sprite wings, and nothing. Anxiety was gnawing at my gut, Graz was still nowhere to be seen and we couldn't hold the launch for her.

I reminded myself that she could take care of herself... so why did I feel like we were abandoning her? Just space me now.

Then just as we arrived at the airlock I asked, "I would have thought Captain Vandross would be here to see us off."

Richter assured me with the same diplomatic face every politician was assigned at birth that indicated there are bigger things to worry about than the mundane, "Captain Vandross has two Cityships to run in my absence, so she is needed in the command center."

There were already dozens of people being loaded as we arrived. All in tattered clothing, some on crutches, and a couple on stretchers. My security detail we had left behind was scanning each person for energy weapons as they were given directions to follow the relief workers to the cargo bay and strap into their cots for launch.

I had so many questions looking at the mix of people. Most of the men and women didn't look as bad off as the ones on stretchers or the two children that were loaded aboard. I knew there were other children with just as bad if not worse radiation burns on them. Why did the group mostly consist of adults?

I had to remind myself, that as alien as their culture seemed to be to me, ours must be just as alien. I would just have thought they'd want their children cared for first.

Sighing I just looked around, and almost jumped out of my skin when Mir said into my ear from behind me somehow, "This is going to be one crowded ship."

I glanced back at her, still dressed in my clothes, and noted her eyes were not on me, they were on the people boarding the ship. Nodding I said, "Yes, it's going to be one interesting ride."

Mother started playing, 'Smoke on the Water', by a band called Deep Purple, from my library. She had a knack for playing songs that matched the turmoil inside of me.

Then Mir said, "See you in a bit, time to play nice-nice." She beamed a smile as she strode away toward the Captain and his security team as they were arguing with my security detachment. I waved them off, Mother relaying to them that the Lancers were allowed to keep their weapons.

Then Mir said as she bowed her head slightly, "Captain Richter, welcome aboard. The master of the Underhill, Mac, has extended an invitation for you to accompany him on the bridge for takeoff."

The man inclined his head as he studied her. "I'd be delighted. AI?"

She sighed and assured him, "Not AI, not android nor robot, I'm human. I just have a significant number of mods." She held out a hand. "Mir." He shook as he looked at her hand as it reflected the world around us.

Then she looped her arm in his and moved them along through the corridor, the Lancers starting to follow until the man made a rough dismissive motion and they stayed behind. I heard him making conversation with Mir. "Mac? Did you know the original master of the AJAX-43 was a man named MacKenzie Carpenter?"

As they turned at an intersection I heard her voice drifting over the murmur of the people still being loaded on board. "A family name passed down over the generations."

I smirked. What were the odds that Mac was likely a dead ringer for this MacKenzie Carpenter?

With that, I exhaled loudly then joined the rest of my squad to help screen patients and get them to the cargo bay with our medical personnel and get them strapped in for launch.

The one bright spot in my day was when I get a woman settled into a cot, and demonstrated the old fashioned belt strap, and I noted three rows away, was the little boy who had given me the twisted metal bird. I beamed a smile at him and waved, he grinned, showing an adorable missing tooth smile and waved back at me.

Good. I remembered my motto from my early days in the brigade that made the rough days livable, "Do just one good thing." This boy was my one good thing for the day.

Chapter 10 – Hangover

That first day was chaos, trying to get a ship full of people into a routine. Mac had made a show of first making an orbit around the Cityships once we launched to give anyone near a window a spectacular view of the giant vessels. Then he gracefully maneuvered through the swarm of banged up vessels that looked to be barely flying and called out on coms, "Mercy Fleet, Underhill. Accelerate to rendezvous speed on my mark. Three, two, one, mark."

He looked at us as and grinned as he slammed the controls forward, pressing us back into our seats. Richter noted, "There's virtually no vibrations in the deck plates. The engines must still be tuned to factory specs. It feels like more than the three Gs of acceleration the AJAX vessels were rated at."

Mac responded with a shrug and a simple, "The Underhill has quite a few surprises in her."

After our burn was completed and Mac started the rotation of the ship to give us some semblance of gravity, he called out on shipwide coms, "That's it boys and girls, feel free to get up and stretch your legs if you'd like, it's going to be a long trip."

Then he hailed the makeshift fleet, "Mercy Fleet, stay in formation, we'll see you on the flip side."

I swear half the time I didn't know the meanings of the archaic expressions the old man threw about.

I keyed in an external view of the Cityships quickly receding into bright points of light and bit my lower lip as the knot in my stomach tightened even more. To my surprise, Delphine stepped up to me and placed her porcelain white hand on mine and said in a low voice, "The Sprite is resourceful. She will be fine."

I nodded and exhaled, then said, "I need to beat the shit out of something. Care to spar after I do my rounds to make sure everyone is good?" Her self assured smile was all I needed to know that she was game.

Delphine and Yar had to actually call out Mir and me, and a couple others from the security team, we were being too aggressive for a sparring match and had them on the ropes, about to start using magic to defend themselves.

I held my hands up in supplication and exhaled as sweat virtually poured off my brow to sizzle on my lower lip. "I'm sorry. We just... the people on the Redemption... they're so... desperate, so, I don't know... beaten? And afraid. Those damn Outliers with their armbands were keeping everyone cowed and..."

I slammed a fist into a bulkhead, my armor sparking against the wall, leaving a mark where I had impacted it. I immediately grabbed my fist and winced. That was going to bruise.

Delphine offered, "And there was nothing you could do about it as you are a hundred million miles or so out of your jurisdiction?"

I pointed at her. "Yes! That!"

Yar offered, "Perhaps the governing body of the Cityships will accept an offer of help from the Brigade in stemming their Outlier problem once they arrive at the world."

I blinked at him and smirked as I said, "You know that's the most you've ever said to me in one sentence since you threatened me at the gates of Verd'real."

He narrowed his eyes. "That can't be right, can it?"

I cocked an eyebrow in challenge. "Mother?"

Mother churned out in a tinny tone, "On your first meeting with Captain Yar, he stated... 'I am the Captain of the Verd'real home guard, you wouldn't dare, and wouldn't get a single step before I ran you...' before you cut him off. Twenty-two words. His earlier statement constituted twenty-seven words."

I added with a grin, "It almost sounds as if you care."

Delphine snorted and shared with him, "I said virtually the same thing on my first meeting with Shade."

He stated matter of factly, "She does tend to have that effect on the people she meets, does she not?"

Now I know they were trying to get a rise out of me but I was just smiling like a lunatic because apparently, all it took to get the two from trying to kill each other and actually start bantering like allies, was a single frustrating Human. And I could frustrate the hells out of most anyone... just ask... most anyone.

Delphine swung at me, and I was already leaning back on instinct as I started backpedaling, ducking blow after blow as she prompted, "Tell us what you've observed thus far. I'm sure you've reviewed the footage of the meetings already."

I spun under a well-executed thrust of her bladed hand and slammed my fist into her armpit as I spun away. Ow! It was like hitting the bulkhead again, but she started favoring that arm. I must have hit the nerve cluster I had been aiming for. She'd heal up in seconds so I'd have to capitalize on it.

Yar asked as I cartwheeled in the air in the light gravity and brought first one then the other leg down on her arms she crossed over her head to absorb the blows, "Footage of the meetings? How did you obtain those?" He sounded almost affronted.

I shrugged and said, "A little birdie, why? Is it that shocking?"

He said as Mir cushioned his fall when she flipped him onto his back when he struck at her from behind and her arms actually folded backward to grab his fist and then hip throw him, "Yes. Those were diplomatic proceedings. If they found you had somehow smuggled in recording equipment to..."

Delphine sighed heavily and cut him off, "Oh loosen your panties, Summer." Then she prompted me as she kicked me halfway across the room, "Did I use your Human colloquialism correctly?"

I shook my head. "It's 'Don't get your panties in a bunch.'"

She sighed like it didn't make sense to her then looked over her shoulder to Yar when they were forced to fight back to back as our other sparing partners joined us, alternating between helping us corner the Fae and attacking us in turn. "Mab's tits man. You must have known how exposed we were when the asinine half-elf sent away the security detachment. It was insurance. I was wearing the Lieutenant's wrist console to the discussions."

He growled and she flipped him over her shoulder, using him as a projectile to take down our Orc and Dwarf. He stood and said in frustration, "I understand operational security, Winter, it's just that there are no recordings allowed in the palaces when the Queens are in discussions with anyone."

I smirked and held up my hands in surrender after the two of them cornered me and I dodged and blocked a flurry of blows, noting how well they fought as a team. "News flash, genius, you weren't in the palace and there was no Queen present. Besides, we can plead ignorance of their customs if push came to shove."

He shook his head as Mir slammed him to the deck and he tapped out. "We could not, as it would be a lie."

My eyes widened. "Would it? Do you know as a fact that they do not allow their meetings to be documented?"

He hesitated as Mir helped him stand again. His brow furrowed. "No, I don't."

"So no lie."

"We could infer..."

Delphine snapped at him, "Oberon's balls man, do you argue just to argue? She stated a truth, whether we believe it to be otherwise, we do not definitively know unless we ask, so her ploy is valid. Worthy of a Fae even. Not bad for a Human."

They started to take a defensive stance again and I shook my head. "Unlike you Fae and some of the other preternaturals here, we humans have a limit. I appreciate you allowing me to beat the shit out of you for a bit. It really helped relieve some of my helpless frustration."

Delphine smirked slyly. "That was dangerously close to a thank you, Shade."

"You wish."

Mir said to me, "Speak for yourself, Knith, I'm not even winded yet."

I whined out, "You don't need to breathe!"

She struck a seductive pose as she said teasingly, "I know, I can go all night."

I muttered to the others, "She's hopeless."

Yar informed her, "You are a most formidable Human opponent. I'd like one day to see how well you'd fare if we could use magic attacks."

Unphased, Mir just winked at me as she said to him, "Can't hurt what you can't hit."

Then the Captain of the Winter Court whispered to me, "Is she always like..."

I nodded. "Yup, pretty much."

And the woman surprised me by asking just loud enough for me to hear, "Why does the master of the Underhill need an assassin close? And who trained her to fight in the old Un'Tchea open hand Fae style?"

I shrugged and whispered back, "I don't know, why don't you ask her?" I had the same question but I wasn't stupid enough to ask. But the little tidbit about it being an old form of Fae combat Mir used was interesting, and just solidified my thoughts on Mac.

Delphine just chuckled. "Do I look like a null or something? I'm not suicidal."

I told the others, "I have to get cleaned up, do my rounds, and call my girl."

Yar muttered to Delphine, "You let her refer to the Winter Maiden as her girl?"

I was grinning like a loon when I heard her countering as the sparring began again behind me, "Nobody lets that Human do anything, she just does."

If I wasn't positive those two would wind up killing each other if they were ever locked in a room with each other, I'd almost swear their constant banter was filled with sexual tension. Now there was an interesting thought.

It was the same type of vibe I got off of Mab and Titania when they were together. Like they were moments from either striking the other down or just tearing each other's clothes off. And a comment Queen Titania made to me when she thought I was Mab during the Firewyrm indecent, alluded to the fact that at one time they had been lovers.

Once I cleaned up... in a sonic shower, really missing a good water shower, but we needed to ration the water right now, I redressed and headed out to check with everyone at their posts and checked to be sure the shifts were all assigned for the tenth time.

When I was in the cargo hold, it struck me as odd. I mean, the medical personnel were moving between the cots, and their voices echoed in the space as they dictated things to the other aid workers. Then I got it. All the people from the Cityships were all still here in the cargo hold in their cots, none were even curious enough to explore this ship, and they weren't even talking among themselves.

I walked over to the senior Med-Mage. "Everything ok in here? It seems too quiet."

The Elf shrugged, then she offered, "I think their ailments are just making them lethargic. Possibly? We don't know much about their culture, so maybe their social interactions vary from ours?"

She was just guessing too.

I looked at the big chrono on the wall and smiled. "Well, I know how to animate them." And right on time, Jane and the quartermaster brought in a large mag-sled that had a table loaded with bowls, spoons, and three large kettles of delicious-smelling soup. They had prepared a chicken broth-based soup with fresh vegetables from Madame Zoe's garden, and dehydrated chicken chunks.

It was simple to prepare for large groups and didn't cut deeply into the limited supplies we had left on the ship. We would only have three meals on a two-day journey back home. Even so, it was likely more food than any of these people had seen in years.

I called out, "For those of you who are mobile, we've soup, just line up here. Aid workers will bring you some if you're not able."

And the last thing I had anticipated happened. Instead of people desperately getting into line to get what little food we had, most just looked around at each other, standing almost leisurely, a few even stretching.

Only two men and a woman, who looked to be in worse shape than the rest, did make their way swiftly to us, with desperate hunger in their eyes. And the two children almost tripped over themselves to get to us.

The rest sort of looked over, then languidly made their way over. I helped hand out bowls and Jane and the Quartermaster, whom I really needed to ask his name without insulting the man by admitting I didn't know it, ladled out generous helpings of soup.

The three didn't even bother getting back to their cots as they sat against the bulkhead and shoveled the hot soup into their mouths as fast as they could cool it on their spoons. The girl looked almost ready to burst into sparkles and rainbows as Jane smiled at her. Fauns had that effect on people. Too cute to not smile at.

Then the madame of the brothel ladled two scoops for her and handed her the bowl. "It's hot, sweetheart. Don't eat it too fast." The girl moved to the other adults long the wall and sat, closing her eyes tight as she just inhaled the steam of the soup and sighed heavily.

Then my smile threatened to split my face when the little boy beamed up at me, tapping his button light on. I inclined my head. "Well hello there little man, we meet again. I'm Knith."

"Lincoln."

I held the bowl out and Jane double ladeled again and I handed him the soup, winked and saluted. "Hello Lincoln, I'm happy to meet you."

The little guy blushed and saluted with the spoon, blurted, "You got pretty lips," and then rushed off to the others to eat.

Jane chuckled. "I think he's smitten."

I pointed at my lips. "No, I think he likes my curses."

"I thought they were the marks from the Queens."

"Trust me, that is a curse."

Then the others moved past, not in any hurry. They moved back to their cots after getting their soup and some just sat it there to cool as they pulled out what looked, to be honest to goodness paper books to read. Why weren't they eating? Weren't they ravenous like the others?

Just like the Cityships, I was starting to get freaked the fuck out there.

I went over to sit by the people at the wall and looked over at Lincoln. He was eating as fast as he could, blowing on the soup. I asked the man near him, "I haven't had a chance to talk to anyone on the Redemption. What is it like living there?"

The man looked from me to the others in the cots. He shook his head. I assured him, "It's ok. I'm just curious if life on the Cityships is like life on the Leviathan."

Looking nervous, he looked back at me and said in hushed tones. "It was better when I was young. Before the insurrection. Before the Outliers reign of terror."

He hesitated then quieter he said, "I remember the tales my parents would share. Of how the people of Earth so many generations ago, saw the launch of the great Worldship the size of the sky. How they were the great hope of mankind that we would be remembered by the new civilization on the faraway planet the Mighty Leviathan was traveling to."

The man spoke like he was relaying a fairy tale, a myth almost forgotten. "Then the great builders, with the ingenuity unmatched, and the last of the resources of mankind, devised a way to use the great stations of the orbiting shipyard into the six Cityships that could join the Worldship on its journey, so more of their descendants might know the new world one day."

He looked at his empty soup bowl. "But as each generation passed, there were those who thought that instead of joining our brothers and sisters on the journey, that it should have been our people instead of yours to have inherited the Mighty Leviathan. That the Fae and other magical creatures had fogged your minds to use you to save themselves."

"They spoke of the Ka'Infinitum, the power of powers that controlled you. And that the Ka'Infinitum was the birthright of the Outliers, who suffered the generations on the Cityships, while the Fae lived in opulence with a ship full of human slaves."

He whispered almost too quietly to hear, "They want the Worldship for their own. Even if it kills us all to get it."

I nodded and asked, "Why haven't your leaders put an end to the Outliers? Why do they let them terrorize your people? I saw them in the crowds on your ship."

People were looking our way now, and he said, "I have to get back to my cot. Thank you for the food. I've not eaten like this since I was a child." Then he was limping back toward the cots.

I looked from him to Lincoln. "Sir, what about your son?"

The man looked back then at the boy, "He isn't mine."

Oh. I looked around the place, I didn't see the woman I had seen him with on the Redemption, so I assumed one of the ones too sick to stand was his father then.

I looked at the boy and winked again as I stood. Then I stepped over to ruffle his hair. "Be a good boy for your dad, I'll see you later when I do my rounds again." He just nodded as he drank the broth from his bowl, giving me a thumbs up with his spoon.

He was going to be a heart-breaker when he grew up, with that shaggy mop of blonde hair. I really hope the Med-Bay back home could repair his eye, or give him a color-matched cybernetic-implant.

After checking with all my team, and then visiting the cockpit to see Mac familiarizing Richter with the upgraded flight controls, I headed to my cabin to make a call before I hit the rack. My turn on the watch was in seven hours.

I checked in with Myra as I walked. She was hissing when Mother opened a channel. "Stupid fucking rock farmers, learn to fly!"

Chuckling I asked, "Everything going ok out there, Kitty Cat?"

"Shade? I'm ten seconds away from spacing myself just so I don't have to keep on these space bumpkins. They have no discipline and are always drifting off course. Those flying cans of space debris weren't meant for precision flying nor space travel. It like herding..."

She trailed off and I giggled. "Herding cats?"

She hissed in a chuckle, "I hate you. But yes, like herding cats... drunk space cats."

Nodding I offered, "I remember a certain drunk space cat who..."

"That's enough of that. Did you ping me just to tug my whiskers and bring up embarrassing college tales? And if I remember right, I wasn't the only one who was too drunk to..."

"Right, changing topics. We going to get this ragtag fleet back home in one piece?"

She yowled and said, "We'll get them there. I may not have any sanity or patience for fools by then, but we'll make it. They don't even have flight computers to slave to my ship so Mother can keep them flying straight."

Nodding as I made it to the cabin I was assigned, I told her, "Well, you've got my number if anything pops up. I'm going to call home then hit the rack for some z's."

She teased, "Oooo, someone's getting some virtual princess nookie."

I offered her a helpful, "Go space yourself, Myra."

"Oh lighten up, Fae Lips, I'm living my sex life vicariously through you and your Winter Maiden."

Shaking my head and feeling the blush burning on my face, I told her, "Hanging up now."

And Mother cut the connection, and I already saw the icon for channel to Rory's lab connecting. I cocked an eyebrow and Mother said, "Oh please, Knith, Commander Udriel isn't the only one living vicariously through your sex life."

My eyes widened at that. Did AI's have a sex life? I mean, I knew she had emotions, and as she had said, she has all the same senses as us except touch. It just struck me as both fascinating to think of the concept of a sentient computer having a sexual identity. Then again, why not? She was a person.

I told her, "Our sex life is none of your business."

Aurora said in a lilting, amused tone, "Then I won't pry."

I blurted, feeling ready to space myself on the sheer principle of it as I spluttered out, "What? No... I... you... she... I was telling Mother to butt out of our sex life."

"Really now?" I could hear the delighted smirk in her tone.

I muttered under my breath, "Oberon's balls."

Then I regained a little composure and said like a smitten schoolgirl, "Hello, Rory. I can't begin to tell you how much I miss you. The Cityships were draining on my humanity and my soul."

She flickered into my vision as Mother activated video. Was my girl blushing? She said, "I've been looking at the reports and the footage Mother has been feeding us." Then she whispered as she said, "I've missed you too, my impulsive Enforcer."

I sat on the bed with my back to the wall and beamed at my girl as Mother started plating an archaeological archives tune called 'Hangover' by Hey Monday. "How was your day, lady?"

We talked and laughed and got lost in each other's eyes and voices as we spoke. It was almost as if I had been going through some sort of withdrawal that was draining away my happiness. But after just a few minutes, I was feeling... well, like me again. This woman was a wonder in more ways than one.

Then I prompted, my curiosity getting the better of me, "So where did you run off to the morning the Underhill launched on the mission?"

Her smile fell and she exhaled audibly and shared, "Mother sent me on a fact-finding mission. Rumors floating around the world about someone gathering classified data on my old experiments in Fae reproduction. Since I'm the only one who could verify anything we found."

That chilled me to the bone, and I had flashbacks of Lord Sindri trying to steal my free will from me and have me kill myself after he had cut my eggs from my body.

She looked around as if someone might be eavesdropping as she gave someone, I assumed her personal guards, a warning glare. Then whispered, "An informant in the Summer Court has shared that Queen Titania is in a rage because someone had broken into Sindri's old labs and had taken all of the documentation on his parallel work months ago."

I whispered, feeling the blood drain from my face, "Is someone trying to duplicate your results?" Her results... that would be me. Her greatest failure and greatest achievement all wrapped up in a Knith shaped bow. I was supposed to have been a Changeling, a half Human, half-Fae to help to repopulate the losses in their population since Exodus.

Static Equilibrium of the population of the Leviathan has been achieved all this time with the exception of the Greater Fae, who have not been able to reproduce since they left the massive wellspring of magic at the heart of the Earth.

Instead of a Changeling, she made... well... a human. What she calls the next evolution of humans, without many of the weaknesses of my race. But the fact that that occurred, and I have partial immunity to magic, she believes that by studying me, she could one day fix what she did and save the future of her race. Only... I don't want to be a guinea pig for the Fae. I'm sure one day I'll be able to look past feeling like a victim after what Sindri had put me through, and look past my own emotions. But today is not that day.

She exhaled loudly, looking distressed as she said quickly, "I'm sorry, I know it causes you distress, I just didn't want to withhold anything when you asked."

I nodded and said, "And that's why I love you, ice geek."

She giggled and said, "Well I love you too. Geek? I'm no geek."

I sighed as we bantered until I had to get some shuteye. Then as we were saying our goodbyes, I let her know about Graz being missing. She muttered something about impulsive Sprites then said, "I'm sure she'll be waiting at the airlock on the next visit. Sleep tight, Knith Shade."

"Good night, Princess."

Chapter 11 – Mac?

I woke just before someone tapped on the door to wake me for my shift. I swung my legs down and started putting on my Tac-gear, pulling my SAs up over the contact points on my skinsuit as I yawned. "Enter," as I checked the charges on my MMGs and looked around for my helmet.

The Orcish woman ducked her head under the doorframe and said, "You left a message on the duty roster to wake you for your shift... ma'am."

I nodded, suppressing another yawn and said, "Thank you, Corporal Tonga is it?"

She huffed with a nod, her nostrils flaring with the exhale almost touched her lower tusk fangs. "Yes, ma'am."

Then I started to the door and she started to turn her impressively muscled bulk toward the corridor when she paused and looked back at me. "Is it true?"

I cocked my head, inviting her to clarify. She looked almost embarrassed asking, "You beat a Greater Fae in combat?"

It was my turn to feel embarrassed. That story keeps circulating, even though I had plenty of help taking Lord Sindri down. Mother and even Mab's magic with the help of the harmonica I carried everywhere. The one Mac gave me that seems to amplify Fae magic flowing through it when played. All that, and I was pissed the hells off.

She confided, "I wouldn't have believed it until LNN News broadcast the wave of you outside on the skin, fighting two skin jockey Mech-Rigs barehanded."

I shook my head. "Everything you heard and saw is taken out of context and you don't know the whole story. There were a lot of extenuating circumstances, and I had a lot of help."

She nodded and said, looking relieved, "Good, because, I mean... you're a human. If you know what I mean."

Sighing, mostly because I really did know what she meant. But it would do her good to be a little wary of humans, so I shamelessly said as I clapped her shoulder as I pushed past into the corridor, "They don't even mention that after that, I had finished my day by challenging the Summer and Winter Queens."

It happened to be a true statement of fact, so I tried hard not to snort when the Orc just peered out of my cabin at me, eyes wide. Then she started shaking her finger at me as she smiled, "You almost had me there, Lieutenant."

I just looked back and cocked an eyebrow at her in a challenge, she furrowed her great brow then prompted, "You were joking right?" I just kept walking as she called out to me a little louder, "Right?"

Mother was in my head. "That wasn't very nice, Knith."

I shrugged and she chirped out, "But it was pretty funny."

"It was, wasn't it?" Then I added, "I kind of like that one, she's got moxie."

Mother agreed. "She does. And I think she may have a little hero worship of you, even though she doesn't know how a Human has been so successful in battle since Orcs are the only race that are almost as strong as the greater Fae."

I had to look at one of my helmet cams and pointed out, "You caught that too? Just how intuitive are you? Does it even compute?"

She just said, "Pluh." Causing me to chuckle out loud. I still believe she modeled her own humor after mine.

Glancing back to see the Orc heading toward the cabin she shared with four others on the security detachment, I wondered how close her kind had come to extinction after the wars with the Elves and Fae over the millennia, now the last handful of them was on the Leviathan. Once we reached our new home, where we didn't have to worry about static Equilibrium, hopefully, they can multiply freely under Open Sky.

I turned back to the task on hand and made my way up to the bridge cockpit to start my rounds. Unsurprisingly, I found Mac, Mir, and Captain Richter talking about the ship's systems, the two Lancers who were awake at this hour were standing in the corner, observing.

I don't think I've seen Mac so animated before. He loved talking old tech with someone who understood his antiquated ship. Though Richter seemed saddened over the modifications Mac has done, especially here on the bridge, as they talked about utility over the purity of the systems.

I sidled up to Mir and sighed. "They still going on about floating junk heaps?"

She spoke out the side of her mouth, "Yup."

Mac didn't even look at me as he pointed a finger my way. "Stow it, Enforcer. Or you can take a long walk out a short airlock."

I grinned toothily his way and said as I held up my hands. "I wouldn't dream of besmirching your precious Underhill's honor."

He finally looked up and shared his patented shit-eating grin, "You'd best remember that, young Knith."

Sighing I said, my voice filled with resignation that I had to get to business, "Anything I need to know while I was sleeping?"

He shook his head. "Regular contact with the world and Ready Squadron... speaking of, excuse me." He opened a com channel. "Hey, cat, wake up! You're up. Your other pilot just signed out for some sleep. You have two drifters."

Myra was on the channel. "What? Huh? I'm up, I'm up! Umm... ok, I'm awake. Drifters?"

Mir chuckled and chimed out for Mac, "Your counterpart isn't as good at corralling the flailing chickens as you. Two are a thousand miles off course, bearing 025 mark 15.3."

She growled out, "Mab's tits, and you're just now telling me?"

Our mirror skinned friend told her, "You needed your beauty sleep, and they are still inside the flight envelope, we would have woke you if there was any danger."

She muttered back, "These wrecks shouldn't be out this far, to begin with, and their pilots don't seem to have any navigation skill or situational awareness. It may as well be Shade flying them."

"Hey now, lady. I can hear you."

She chuckled and said, "I thought I heard you breathing there. I stand by my words."

I shook my head and muttered, "Cats." Then gave everyone a sloppy salute. "Well I'm off on rounds, call if anything interesting happens."

And then what felt like the most boring day of my life began as I started walking my rounds, checking on all the others on the same security shift as mine.

The only bright spot was that Jane and Madame Zoe used up all the supplies we had left, and what fresh greens the Clairvoyant could spare for huge lunch since we would be docked on the Leviathan before the Day Lights went out for the night on the world.

I tried to catch Lincoln for lunch, but all the Cityshippers opted to stay in their bunks this time with their meals. The man I had spoken with before looked almost afraid.

We were just a couple hours out from the Leviathan, seeing it growing brighter on the screens when I saw one of our security men hauling one of the four Lancers bodily to the old brig just outside the cargo hold.

I made my way there quickly. "What's going on here?"

The Elf looked at me and said, "I was just about to call you, Lieutenant. I caught this man in the off-limits area in environmental control. He refuses to explain why he was skulking around in there."

I hit the com panel on the side of the door as I looked through the blast glass at him. "What were you doing in environmental control?"

He didn't even acknowledge me. I sighed and dropped my hand from the panel. "Send beta squad to check out Environmental Control and also, see how he got into a secure area. I'll get Captain Richter down here, maybe he can get his man to talk."

The Elf nodded. "Yes, Lieutenant."

Then before I could ask, a connection was pinging to the bridge, Mac said, "What is it Shade?"

"Hello to you too, you stale space fart. We've got a problem with one of the two Lancers that were supposed to be in their rack. He was sniffing around Environmental and won't speak to us, could you see if Richter can get him talking?"

Captain Richter responded, "On my way down, Lieutenant Shade." Then he was saying, "I hate incompetence. Care to join me, Mac?"

"Of course. Be right down, Knith."

I absently nodded then made my way back out into the cargo hold to wait by the ladders, since I knew Mac wouldn't use the lift. I glanced around the space and smiled, in just a couple short hours, these people were going to get the proper medical treatment they were in dire need of.

Mir slid down the rails then Mac and Richter followed with his two Lancers in tow. Mir fell in beside me as Captain Richter furrowed his brow as he looked to the side as we started to walk and said, "What was that there?" He moved to a small maintenance airlock Mac at his side, scanning the airlock to see what Richter was talking about.

Then chaos ensued.

In one quick motion, Richter pushed Mac into the airlock, lifted the emergency venting cover and slammed the red button. My eyes widened in horror as I heard myself screaming, "No!"

Mir's arms were shiny blades in an instant as I drew my twin MMG's on reflex. I was barely aware that almost everyone in the cargo hold, including Richter, pulled out flimsy filter masks as the fog started spewing from the air vents.

My fingers were starting to squeeze the triggers, and Richter started to go down as one of the tiny darts struck him and channeled a stunning blast into him. And I looked down as something hit my feet while Mir started to dive at the crumpling man, screaming in anguish and rage, what was that round...

There was a bright flash and Mir dropped like a marionette whose strings had been cut. My MMG's and armor went dead in the same instant. Was that some sort of an EMP grenade?

I dropped my MMG's and grabbed my twin cold iron batons, flicking them out as I dove at the Lancers as they opened fire on me. I was feeling sluggish, and their projectile weapons hammered at my armor. Even unpowered, it was a match for the weapons, even though I felt like I was being pounded by a series of hammers.

Staggering, as I felt woozy like I had been on an all-night drinking binge. I swung low, shattering one man's kneecap, but I followed my strike down, my helmet bouncing off the floor. I felt like I was made of lead as I tried to lift my arms.

Far too late I realized that it was some sort of gas being pumped into the ship as my eyesight blurred then the fog took over my brain as the world folded in on me into darkness. The last horrified thought I was capable of thinking before I was out, was, "Mac?"

Chapter 12 – Under Pressure

I don't know how long I was out, but when I came to, it felt as if I had been trampled in a cattle stampede in the B-Rings. My extremities were tingling as I fought off the last of the effects from the gas.

I used my anger and sorrow over losing Mac to the harsh vacuum of space to clear my head. I realized my cheeks were wet with tears. I sat up, feeling the aches and pains from the beating I took from the projectile weapons as well as what felt like a physical beating while I was down and out. I found I was in only my skinsuit, all my gear had been stripped from me.

One arm looked to be soaked in blood where a projectile had torn through my armor and grazed me, but my healing factor had already stemmed the bleeding and it was already scabbing over.

Wiping the tears, I scrambled to one of the bodies on the floor near me. Her mirrored skin looking inanimate scared the hells out of me. Mir always looked so... alive, even with her full body cyber mods. But now she almost didn't look real with her eyes staring blankly at the wall where her head was pointing.

She didn't breathe so I had no idea if she were... dead or not. EMP grenades were outlawed on space faring vehicles even prior to the construction of the Worldship, in the last war mankind waged between the Mars and Lunar colonies and Earth. Mostly because an EMP large enough could doom an entire ship, condemning all souls on board to the excruciating pain of suffocation or freezing to death without life support. It had been considered cruel and unusual by the Fifth Geneva Accords.

But that was how they took out both Mir and my Scatter Armor before I could drop my visor. It effectively disabled my MMGs as well. That gas they pumped through the environmental systems finished me off.

I turned Mir onto her back and just prayed that hers was a legal augment since full body augments were required by regulations to have a biological backup in case of system or power failure. But for all I knew, my friend, like Mac, was dead.

I looked up and called out, "Mother?" She'd be able to scan her.

A voice against the wall said, "Don't bother. They disabled all com links when they gassed us." I glanced over to see the other human Enforcer holding her bloodied cheek. She looked as if she had been beat half to death. I looked from her to the others and went around taking pulses of the few Humans of Mac's Crew, the relief workers, and a small number of Cityshippers, then scrambled with a panic to an unconscious Lincoln when I saw his little body laying limp behind a man.

The Enforcer offered, "All alive." I sighed out in relief as I arranged Lincoln to a more comfortable position on the deck.

Closing my eyes I put it all together, and was wondering how we hadn't before. I mean, we were all feeling things were off. It all seemed obvious now. Richter and the Lancers were Outliers. They controlled the Cityships. They wore the same blue and greens as the Outliers with the armbands. They had carefully planned this out to take Mac's ship for some reason, that's why they knew so much about AJAX vessels.

What was the endgame though? What had that other man in the cargo bay... who was now in here with us, said? Something about the Ka'Infinitum being the birthright of the Outliers, who suffered the generations on the Cityships, while the Fae lived in opulence with a ship full of human slaves.

Were they really going to try to take the Ka'Infinitum? What did they believe that would accomplish?

I felt the blood drain from my face as I scrambled to the other woman and started checking out her wounds. My eyes widened when I noted both of her legs were sitting at unnatural angles. I looked at her as she hissed while I felt along her skinsuit. One knee was dislocated, and the other leg was broken.

I looked her in the eye and said as I lifted her leg and placed my hands strategically, "Private?"

She looked away from my hands, pain evident on her face. "Ma'am." And without warning I bent her knee joint back down toward her body and heard a popping crunch and she screamed as I popped her knee back in place.

Patting her shoulder I said, "Good job."

She looked on the verge of passing out now, but she said between gritted teeth, trying to make light of it. "Give a girl some warning next time."

I shook my head, "Then you would have resisted whether you meant to or not." I grabbed a blanket off of a cot welded onto the wall and started biting it and tearing it into strips. I looked around and then started kicking out at one of the legs of the welded cot. It broke free after the fifth kick. My entire body shook in pained shock with every impact, reminding me I wasn't in much better shape than her.

Then I used the short pipe and the strips to splint her other leg. She hissed in pain multiple times as I worked. I tried to keep her mind off the pain. "They really did a number on you."

She chuckled, and a blush appeared on her deathly pale face, "I think I did this to myself." She waved a hand at her legs. "When the gas started coming from the vents, I got my visor up and I started for the bridge, but men rushed up from the lower levels and there was some sort of flash-bang then my armor powered down. I fought, but it was a losing proposition, so I was going to go for help at the cargo bay."

"I leapt down the engineering conduit three floors, forgetting my armor wasn't powered anymore. That's the last thing I remembered until I woke up in here, with them throwing people and you in here... the fucking bastards took my armor."

I nodded and said, "They have EMP grenades, that's what took out Mir and my armor."

Her eyes widened in shock. "But EMPs are outlawed."

I shrugged. "Yet here we are." Then I asked as I looked around, seeing only Humans, getting a really bad feeling, "What about the others?"

She shook her head, "I don't know. I couldn't pull myself up to see out the brig window."

I stood and made my way to the door and looked out. Strewn about in the corridor was our armor and gear. It took ten minutes from a critical failure for the magi-tech systems to reboot our armor systems.

So I asked as I realized something didn't feel right about the ship. Then I realized it was because we were decelerating and our spin was arresting as we slowly lost gravity. I blurted, "How long have I been out?"

She shrugged, "Maybe two hours?"

Mother fairy humper, we had arrived at the Leviathan. As gravity lost its hold on us, I pushed myself to the people scattered about, starting to free float and said, "Tear more strips." She looked at me then them and nodded.

We went about strapping the people to the cots around the walls. Then I floated back to the door. We needed to get out of here now and stop this madness before more people got hurt. She was now mobile in zero gravity and she asked, "What are we going to do?"

I looked around. There had to be a way to get out. But the brig was built extremely well. Not even an access panel on the inside. I pushed off and grabbed one of the light fixtures, placing my feet on the ceiling on either side of it and strained. With a protesting groan of metal, the casing bent away just when my straining muscles felt ready to tear.

The Enforcer blinked. "Do you have more mods than just your lips?"

I shook my head, "I don't have any mods. These are the marks of the Winter and Summer Queen. I'm just strong for my size."

I reached inside the fixture and was disappointed that there weren't any plasma relays, and no capacitance crystals I could discharge like a makeshift cutting torch. The lights were powered by honest to goodness electron flow through metal conductors? Was that done anymore? Then I remembered the age of the ship. Mac hadn't gotten around to replacing the power systems it appears.

I felt a pang in my heart at the thought about the loss of the rebellious Remnant captain. Pulling out the wires to the maximum, I asked, "What's your name?"

She looked stricken and resigned as she said, "Audrey Jameson."

I told her with apology in my tone for not remembering, but in my defense, there were too many new faces on the roster for the mission and I hadn't memorized them, "Ok stay away from the door, Jameson." Then I jammed the exposed wires on the door and sighed when they sparked and nothing happened.

I looked at her and said, "Ok, that about exhausts my extensive list of ideas. Do you have any?"

She blinked, likely wondering how I could joke at a time like this. Then she shook her head. We both spun in the air when Mother said from behind us, "I have an idea Knith, why don't I open it?"

My jaw hung open when I saw Mir standing behind us, her feet melding with the deck plates, a silly crooked grin on her face. Her body language was all wrong as she cocked her head at me, studying me like she had never seen me before.

"Mir?"

"No, silly, her software is re-training, she'll be back with us in a minute or two. Good thing she had bio-backup systems to keep her brain alive."

"Mother?" It was beyond freaky hearing Mother's voice coming from Mir's mouth.

She nodded, "Of course. When the Mercy Fleet started attacking the upper rings and I realized all com channels in the Underhill were disabled, and I couldn't rise anyone's wrist consoles or SAs, that you might need my help." Mabs tits! The stacks were under attack?

Then she held her hands in front of her and flexed her fingers as she stared in almost childlike wonder, "So this is what touch feels like." She ran a hand along her arm. Then she looked up at me, "As Mir's systems started rebooting, I took control over the data channel. But as soon as she is conscious, I'll be blocked out, her brain being sort of the ultimate wetware firewall."

She stepped past me as I pulled myself down to the floor using a handrail. She paused and smiled at me in wonder and reached a hand out to tentatively run her fingertips along my cheek and jaw. Then she looked at her fingers, shaking her head. "I've never had input like this. It is incredible."

Then she looked at us, "You may want to stand back." We moved aside along the grab rails and she held her hands up and looked at both sides of them and said, "Fascinating," as they flattened and reformed into blades. Then she punched the window. Even though it wasn't blast-glass, it was about three inches thick and vacuum rated, but she blew a hole into it.

Then she grinned at me and bit her silver tongue as an arm elongated reaching out through the hole and she squinted an eye and looked up as she reached for something on the other side. A moment later the door cycled open as she pulled her arm back. "There. Now, I would suggest gearing back up because I can feel Mir pushing against my control. She's starting to wake up."

It was still odd hearing Mother's voice coming from Mir, but I told her, "You're amazing, Mother. You've always got my back."

She nodded as she looked at her hands again in wonder, flexing them, "Always." Then as I started to the corridor to get back into my Scatter Armor like Audrey was doing as she pulled off the makeshift splint. I was going to tell her not to, but then realized the armor would splint her leg better and give her full mobility back.

I looked at the ragged tear in the arm of my SAs, where the projectile had compromised it, and watched as the nano-panels reconfigured, sealing the damage.

Before I could pull myself out the door, Mother stopped me. "Wait. I may never get another chance, and I've always wondered."

I opened my mouth to ask, "Wondered what?" but found her kissing me tenderly instead. My eyes widened in shock and surprise, but then her body shifted subtly and she started kissing me more aggressively. I pulled away and a familiar smarmy smirk was on her lips as Mir said, "Wow, what a way to wake up. Didn't know you swung the cyber-way, Knith."

Sighing, I shook my head, "Get your brain out of the gutter, mirror-girl. We have a ship to take back."

Then she froze and I saw the moment she remembered what happened to Mac as her face was painted in loss and rage. "These fucking sons of bitches are going down!"

The moment I was geared up, my mag boots engaged and helmet on with visor locked, I said almost desperately as the suit went into self diagnostic mode. "Mother?"

"Here, Knith."

I had never been so relieved to hear someone's voice. I got mostly green lights down the board... good enough. Then I looked to Jameson and Mir, "Let's do this."

They nodded, then Mir asked almost sheepishly, "Umm, Knith? Why were we kissing? I thought I was dead when my world went black. Then when I woke..."

I told her, "Long story, sort of busy now. We need to get to the bridge. Quickest route?"

We could hear men down the corridor. It sounded like they were gearing up for something and I was silently glad they hadn't heard the window on the door break.

Mir scowled toward the cargo bay, then turned to the dead end of the corridor and mouthed, "This way."

I looked at the brig then back toward the voices, whispering, "Jameson."

She followed my eyes then whispered back, "But, I want a piece of the hijackers, Lieutenant." There was no way I was leaving defenseless and unconscious innocents undefended. And I didn't want to chance our escape being discovered and the others paying the price for it.

I replied, "The civilians need our protection, that is our number one creed."

She muttered the creed, "Defend the defenseless. Gods be damned."

She slipped back into the brig, and we shut the door. Then Mir stared at the door control pad and it went red as she told me, "Crypto locked, nobody is getting in there unless I transmit the unlock code." To punctuate her words, a steel shutter came down over the broken window.

I cut my external speakers and said on our tac-channel, "Ok, Jameson. Ping me when everyone is conscious, and we'll call the all clear when we draw the sons of bitches out. We're counting on you to get the civilians out safely when we dock. We'll locate the relief workers and the rest of the security team and join you once we secure the bridge."

"Godspeed, Lieutenant."

Then I looked at Mir, who asked me, "How bad is it?"

I shrugged, "I went down when you did. What I don't get is that we were kept alive at all and that the civilians are too. Mother says their mining ships are attacking the upper rings." I winced at her glare, knowing she was thinking about Mac again.

I looked at my wrist console, "Mother?"

She displayed views of the Leviathan from the Ready Squadron, who were engaging all the mining vessels which looked to be inflicting an alarming amount of damage on the Alpha and Beta Rings. But they were being systematically wiped out by the superior ships of the Squadron.

More views came up of men in antique vac-suits clomping along the skin, firing projectiles at the Brigade Enforcers who were exiting airlocks to engage them. Again, the enemy was greatly outmatched.

Mir hissed in satisfaction, but I started shaking my head. She prompted, "What is it? They're getting their asses handed to them."

I looked at her and said, "It's a diversion. They aren't expected to win, just to keep our forces busy while the rest go for the trunk with the Underhill. They're after the Ka'Infinitum, but they don't understand what it is. Their whole cause is based on the predication that the objects of power enslave us to the Fae, that it has some sort of magical control over us Humans. They think that with its power they can take over the Leviathan."

She looked at me, her mirrored brow furrowing, "You can't be serious. Are they insane?"

I shrugged. "That or misguided. It is all a myth, a legend to them, almost a religion."

She nodded slowly then said in a dangerous tone, "Well, misguided or not. I'm going to end that murdering bastard who killed Mac."

I should have possibly warned her against that course of action had we been on the world, but the law didn't apply to the Remnants. And I wasn't going to stop her if she got the chance, after what Richter did to Mac. A little voice in the back of my head reminded me that he was likely more than he pretended to be. And that Sindri had survived his spacing because he was Fae, and they didn't die in space, only froze. Could we maybe... locate his body before we got out of range?

I made an ushering motion instead, and she turned and grabbed a maintenance hatch and pulled it off to and sent it drifting down the corridor. "After you."

Mother started playing a song called Under Pressure by another old royal, a Queen.

Nodding I ducked through and looked up the maintenance tube with the ladder leading up multiple levels. She asked from behind me as I crouched, "So, you going to tell me why we were kissing? Was it a Cinderella or Sleeping Beauty kind of thing?"

I glanced over, my face screwed up in confusion, "A cinder-what? No, it was Mother kissing me." Then leapt with all my strength and the servos of my armor, leaving her confused expression behind me as I rocketed up the access shaft.

Looking down I saw her gliding up after me, determination on her face. I caught flashes of the guts of the ship as they streaked past on cross corridors. When I reached the top, at a panel marked Command Control, I grabbed a ladder rung and stopped myself from hitting the top of the shaft.

Mir looked almost like an angel gliding through a golden pond as she gracefully slowed herself with a hand on the ladder as she came to a stop beside me like it was the easiest thing in the world. I muttered under my breath to her with a smirk, "Show off."

She whispered primly, "Not all of us are bumbling brutes."

"Hey."

She grinned and then reached out to slowly, soundlessly, open the access panel a crack. Then the ship shuddered and the sound of docking clamps engaging echoed, metal groaning in protest as the Underhill shook violently for the long eternity of two heartbeats before settling.

I could just see a Lancer by the Captain's chair, where Richter was gripping the manual controls for dear life while the man said to him, "Gods, Richter. Nice fucking docking."

"And you could do better, Smitty? These aren't the flight controls the AJAX was supposed to have, I had to improvise. We have a hard seal. Time to go to work."

Then he hit ships coms, "Ok people go go go, plow the road for us. Kill the roaches, we only get one chance. For humankind!"

The response echoed though the ship even without the intercom amplifying it, "For humankind!"

I was about to burst out and bind them by law when I heard many mag-booted footsteps on the deck-plates beyond. The two were not alone. Then Richter pulled something out of his pack and tossed it, tumbling in zero gravity to the Lancer.

My blood ran cold when I saw it was Graz, in some sort of jar, and Richter said, "Space this one out the nearest airlock, we don't need the filthy thing for leverage anymore. It can join all the other roaches in hard vacuum."

What? I was processing that, but my need to help Graz was foremost in my... In a single motion, Mir had the access door moved aside, and one bladed arm through the Lancer's back, and she caught the jar and dove back toward me before it all registered to the Outliers.

She was yelling, "Go!" As projectiles started ricocheting everywhere, control panels sparking and exploding as I shoved Mir down then yanked myself down to glide down to the next level with her and our trapped friend.

I could hear Richter roaring, "Stop you idiots! You're going to get us all killed before we can finish our mission. Once we get onto the Worldship, get the other humans off the boat and blow it for all I care."

I glanced up the tube from the cross maintenance corridor, to see a red faced Richter in his Vac suit glaring down at us. He slammed his helmet on as he backed away. "They're on the next level down. Keep them there until we get our people off the ship."

Mir said, "Time to skedaddle." And she punched out an access door and we pulled ourselves out into the main level where Mac's cabin was.

Graz was pounding on the glass of the jar yelling something that was too muffled to hear. I held up a stalling finger as I activated my mag-boots while Mir crawled like a mirrored praying mantis along the wall, almost blending in.

We passed by Mac's cabin, and I knew where we were heading, to the main airlock on this level. Mir could survive in space and my suit afforded me more than the thirty minutes it used to as it had a re-breather oxygen canister now, thanks to my notes on this experimental armor. I could be out in vacuum for an hour now.

We heard the lift doors starting to open as we were almost to Madame Zoe's cabin. My blood ran cold. All the other humans were in the brig, but she wasn't, had they... It was all I could do to stop from squeaking in alarm when two hands reached out and grabbed Mir and me and pulled us into a small room that had lattices of plants climbing all the walls. Madame Zoe's hydroponics garden.

I looked to see it had been Jane who pulled us into the space, putting a finger to her lips. Then we heard mag-boots clomping heavily at a run. Madame Zoe was standing at the open door and I almost yelled out to her but the men all ran past. One ordering, "Check all the cabins, they can't have gotten very far. Sweep the next two levels too."

The man shouting orders stopped not two feet from the clairvoyant and looked around, then growled in frustration and followed the others. The old woman said in a pleased tone, "That should do it, they'll be chasing their tails for a while now. Hello ladies."

How? What? Then my eyes widened. Clairvoyants were witches... could human witches cast 'don't look here' spells? I waved absently then sputtered, "Graz!" as my visor snicked up and I reached out to Mir who was hugging first Jane then Zoe. She handed me the jar as I held an arm out and she hugged me, but you couldn't pay me to hug a witch. Zoe still freaked me out.

I looked at the frantic Sprite in what looked to be some sort of honest to goodness jam or jelly jar. I twisted the metal lid she was keeping away from, and the moment I pulled it off, in a streak of sparkling light and dust, Graz was inside my helmet, hugging my neck like her life depended on it. "Oh thank Mab and Titania you saved me, Knith! I thought I was a gonner. They made me watch..."

She sounded horrified and emotionally compromised as her tone conveyed a haunted anguish. "They made me watch as they spaced them... they spaced them all. They knocked them all out with gas and the mother fairy humpers just spaced them in cold blood."

I knew that I had already instinctively known, but didn't want to. I asked slowly, "Spaced who?"

She sounded heartbroken as she said in a hoarse squeak, "Anyone who wasn't human. They called them roaches, monsters, and they just killed them all. Richter had any humans brought to the brig because 'we don't kill our own.'"

We all just stood in stunned silence, processing it. All the relief workers, the doctors, everyone who came to lend the Cityships aid... all dead. All because they were preternatural? My security crew. These fucking Outliers were purists... the worst kind of fanatic. They needed to be stopped... now.

Jane slumped against the wall then asked with hope in her eyes, "Mac?"

I shook my head. "Richter spaced him."

Zoe looked at us like we were stupid, shook her head and repeated what she had said to Mac while her eyes clouded white, "The father is exposed."

We took a minute to get reports from Jane and Graz. They all painted the same picture. Graz learned of the Outliers' plans and of their mutiny to control the Cityships. It was the Outliers' war, not the ships breaking down that left them with only two. For all their grand talk about doing this all for humankind, they've taken tens of thousands of lives themselves. They were the monsters, and they couldn't see that.

When she was going to fly back to warn us all, that's when they caught her. They closed all the vents so she couldn't escape. But she says she blinded five of them before Richter slammed the jar down over her.

Jane moved to a console on the wall and tapped something in. We saw the cargo hold, and Richter followed the last of the men there out the lower airlock that was docked on the trunk. Then she went deck by deck to see only the search crew, six men were left going deck by deck.

I leaned in when the cockpit was shown to be empty. The ship groaned and swayed as the docking clamps detached and the Underhill started to free float. Hells! Richter was ensuring we couldn't follow.

Exhaling in frustration I looked around. "Mir, get to the bridge, vent the deck the Outlier mutineers are on to space, then fly everyone to safety on an airlock on a C or D Ring. I'm going after Richter." No more playing nice.

She started to ask, "How are..."

My glare got her saluting like an ass and saying, "Aye aye, Cap'n."

Graz growled out in a tone thirsty for revenge, "I'm comin' with ya, Knith." Then she said, "I knew you'd save me."

Mir held up a hand, "Hello? I was the one who saved your runty little ass."

"What is it with you humans and my ass? I mean, I know it's an awesome ass but, you're Bigs."

I looked at Jane, "Take care of Zoe, and when Mir gives the all clear, there are a bunch of human civilians down in the brig that need medical attention."

She looked worried, her big doe eyes wide, "Be careful, Knith. These people don't have any problems killing anyone who gets in the way of their holy quest."

I nodded, my visor snicking down as my armor reconfigured for vacuum EVA. I pulled my MMGs that remained accessible as well as my pouches; another request I made when that lack of access almost got me killed; and I assured her as I spun the weapons and headed toward the door, "They won't see me coming."

Chapter 13 – Back In Black

I reached the airlock at the end of the hall and looked back to see Mir heading to the ladder to the bridge, we exchanged silent nods, then I cycled the door.

Graz was pressing herself against my visor looking out as she prompted, "Umm... Knith, you do know the airlock they used was at the bottom of the ship? And that that excrement head detached the ship and we're drifting?"

I nodded and corrected her. "Shithead, Graz. And yes, I know."

She said nervously, "Good... just as long as you know. Because then you won't do anything... you know, Knith-y."

I asked once the airlock finished decompressing and I opened the outer door, sending the warning lights strobing. "I wouldn't do that now would I?"

"Yes. You would."

I shrugged and said, "Ok." Then I pushed off, sending us drifting down toward the Trunk so far below us.

She was screaming at me, "You crazy Big! We're gonna diiiiiiiii... wait, what's the difference between excrement head and shithead?"

"Style and flair."

"Oh, ok... iiiiiiiiiiiieeeeeeeeee!"

We hit the skin, maybe a little too fast and hard as my armor servos protested with my muscles, and I stumbled once but my mag boots held. My noisy helmet-mate looked back to me and said, "Oh, that wasn't so bad. Home sweet home, can we go inside now?"

I said, "I don't think so."

She looked at me then followed my eyes first up to see explosions in space far above as Ready Squadron picked off the mining vessels that were slinging industrial laser fire back at them, the stray shots causing collateral damage on the upper rings.

I even saw the twinkling of debris where some of the honeycomb of grid-work and massive, multilayered, clear armored panels of the sky and its Day Lights were blown out, and what looked to be some debris sucked out in the decompression, but shimmering blue ice covered the holes... Queen Mab's work.

It was like the stories of the end times, where the peoples of the world would be judged by flame and virtue. I only hope we were found worthy by whatever gods were watching.

Then Graz followed my glare from there to the airlock a hundred yards away, where ten men in archaic vac suits waited, weapons drawn. And behind them? Three of the mining ships, their dynamo's spinning up to charge their lasers.

I muttered, "Mother," as I checked the charges on my MMGs, "How about something appropriate here?"

Another song from the anthropological archives started playing, 'Back In Black' by AC/DC, and with a thought, it was blaring as my muscles tensed. Then I charged shouting and broadcasting on the open frequency, "Bring it!"

Graz leaned forward, a look of anticipation and anger on her face as the men started firing. I saw flashes of combustion from the barrels of their weapons as projectiles started flying past. Whatever they used to sling the metal slugs seemed to be some sort of percussive chemical reaction that had its own oxidizer to work in a vacuum.

I roared a challenge as they started to range me, their fire becoming more accurate, but in EVA mode, my armor could handle micro-meteoroids. It still hurt like hells as I leaned into the barrage as they finally had me. It was like being hit by a sledgehammer, over and over.

One leveled a huge gun at me with spinning barrels and rained down hellfire on me, two of the much larger projectiles getting through, one sending searing agony across my side, and one tearing a chunk out of the armor on my leg, and my thigh. I ignored the pain as the suit's systems sealed the breaches and put pressure on the wounds, as I felt Synth-Skin patches being applied.

I closed the range to fifty yards, gritting my teeth through the dizziness and nausea, and started firing my MMGs back at them. The Outliers hesitated and stopped firing when three of them started convulsing and went limp as the magic backed stunners did their work.

I heard over their com channel, "Fuck! Mow her down! We have to buy Richter time." And the three mining ships rocketed forward, burning reaction fuel at full throttle. I ran faster toward them, holstering my guns as they'd be useless against these ships, I was roaring as I reached into one of my belt pouches.

Graz was yelling over the music and my challenge to the ships. "Umm, Knith? Knith? Mother fairy humper!"

I was blown backward, tumbling along the skin by a shock wave when two of the vessels exploded into flying debris after massive electrical discharges hit them from behind me. It was like coherent lightning. I was able to grab a sensor platform, straining my arm until I got my magnetized boots back down to attach to the Skin.

I spun back to see what hit them, and my eyes widened as my heart started hammering in my chest as I saw the impossible. With eyes glowing with brilliant power, and lightning coursing all around his body, striding forward along the Trunk like some long-forgotten god of thunder come to take the souls of the wretched, was Mac!

He turned and thrust a hand up, and unrestrained power shot forward, another beam of coherent lightning slashed through space, tearing a mining ship in half that was firing on the B-Ring so far above.

My instincts had me spinning and leaping at the last second as the third ship that was bearing down on me reached us. Graz was screaming again as I almost cleared the ship, taking a glancing blow that tore some armor off my side.

I released what I was holding as we slid across the hull of the vessel. Just before we spun off into space, my side screaming in pain as the armor sealed and more Synth-Skin patches were applied, I shouted to Mother, "Lockdown!" It felt like I lost a rib or two as I found it hard to breathe.

I caught a glance of the mining ship being yanked down to collide with the Skin, all four of my mag-bands activating, pulling down with a combined forty G's of force. And light bloomed as it exploded.

I got my bearings as we spun. This time, I was prepared for this and was starting to reach for the emergency hyper-compressed gas canister in my belt packs to arrest our spin and guide us back to the Skin, but something grabbed me. My armor was sparking everywhere, telling me it was magic in nature and my Scatter Armor was trying to dissipate the magic, but the source was overwhelming and we stopped spinning and were lowered gently to the Trunk.

I looked back and Mac was almost up to us. He spoke... we were in a god be damned vacuum, and he spoke, and I heard him clear as day as he said, "I'll clean up out here. You go get that mortal son of a bitch."

I just gaped at him, ignoring the projectiles that were zeroing in on us again. Mac was alive... and by what he was doing now, everything I ever thought about him was confirmed. I was excited and relieved and in complete awe because of the power he was wreathed in and how much power he was just throwing around. He had somehow covered thousands of miles of space and was walking along the Trunk in hard vacuum and wasn't freezing.

Graz whispered in complete awe, "Oberon..."

I said, knowing Mac could hear me somehow, "There's no undoing this now, no going back. Everyone will know."

He looked resigned as he lashed out past me and I heard men screaming on the Outlier channel as the incoming fire stopped. "I know, now go."

Madame Zoe's words echoed in my head. The father is exposed. And it still freaked me the hells out.

I nodded once to him, looking into eyes that seemed to have no end, magic crackling in their depths. Then I turned away and started running toward the airlock, my mag-boots clumping, a smile growing on my lips. Mac was alive!

Graz kept trying to look behind us, but the visor wouldn't let her. She seemed to sigh in resignation and then turned her attention to the task on hand. She looked up at me one last time and asked, "Umm... Knith, did you really just takedown a whole spaceship with those souped-up restraints of yours?"

I nodded. "Uh-huh."

She grinned up at me. "You really are a special kind of crazy."

"That's the general consensus."

A man stepped up out of the airlock and started to raise one of those multi-barrel weapons. I grabbed a baton from my hip and tossed it cross-hand with all the augmented strength my arm and suit could muster, and hissed, wincing in pain, my ribs and arm twinging from the effort. A moment later, the baton smashed the honest to goodness glass of his helmet, cutting short his gurgling scream as his air vented.

I grabbed the baton from where it stuck out of his helmet as we passed, his flailing arms going still, then I slid it back into its place on my hip. Graz whistled. "Crazy, and sort of scary."

I flipped us down and around using the grab rails inside the airlock then cycled the doors shut. Once the space was pressurized, my armor reconfigured to its default form, and my visor snicked up, Graz flew out and drew her pointy piece of metal alloy she used as a knife. I checked my vitals. Between the Underhill and the Outliers on the Trunk here, I was pretty beat to shit. But Richter wasn't going to wait around while I whined about my injuries.

With a nod to Graz, which she returned, I cycled the inner door and we moved out into the aftermath of a battle. Bodies and blood were floating around in the corridor everywhere.

I asked, "Mother?"

She played the footage of boarding parties being fought in the stacks and here in the trunk. The Worldship had been taken completely by surprise and there weren't many security personnel down here, and the Outliers just laid waste to the workers and civilians in the space... even the Humans. So much for their edict about not harming their own when they were this close to their goal.

I watched them using those damn EMP grenades before the few Brigade personnel had known what was going on and their armor powered down. They hadn't stood a chance when Richter's small army started spraying projectiles indiscriminately. Oberon's balls!

Mother highlighted a few Outlier corpses in the macabre scene floating before me, then displayed numbers. They still had fifty-five men leading the mutineer captain. It infuriated me that they had played us so well, and had used the Underhill as a troop transport. Of course, our scans of their gear hadn't reveled their weapons, since we scanned for energy weapons, not something as primitive and dangerous to a space vessel as projectile weapons.

I shuddered to think about the damage to the world I had seen outside, and prayed to whatever deity might be listening that we could recover from it. Images of the people in the Cityships sparked through my thoughts.

I grabbed a handrail and yanked myself forward at a faster pace than I could run with my mag-boots. A streak of dark light and dull dust at my side. I've never seen Graz so incensed before. I asked, "You got your head screwed on straight? We have to go into the fight with a level head."

She growled through clenched teeth, "Yeah, yeah, I'm good. But, these fairy brained jerk holes are gonna pay." She pointed around at the bodies we passed. "They're killing my Bigs, and nobody kills my Bigs!"

You would think that such a tiny, lesser Fae, making threats like that would be comical, but... I swallowed. I knew what sort of damage she could do with that little blade of hers, and admitted that it was a good threat.

I drew my MMGs and checked the charge. One was fritzing a bit. Probably because of the EMP grenade. It was a little wonky up on the Skin too, but it looked to be bleeding power. Maybe I can check with Magi-Tech to see if they can imbue a charm in them and my armor to withstand an EMP in the future. Not that it would ever be likely to ever happen again.

Though that was the point, what were the odds it would ever have happened this time? Just because we played by the rules, didn't mean everyone else did.

I slapped the weapon on my leg and the charge went up to ninety percent. Ok, not good to be wielding a weapon that may or may not give out on you in a firefight. I holstered it and pulled out a baton, snicking it out to full length. Sometimes low tech is the best tech, nothing to go wrong.

Graz asked as I floated down the Trunk, "What would it take for an erstwhile Sprite to get a miniaturized MMG?"

Snorting I told her, "Graduate the Brigade Enforcer Academy. Otherwise owning one would see you bound by law and working the mines. Energy or weapon possession is a felony unless you're a palace guard in the Seelie or Unseelie courts."

She parried, "Oooo that Enforcer stuff is for you Bigs, but a palace guard? I've got connections now."

"Your only connection is Rory, and she's my connection, not yours."

"Potato banana. It's all semantics."

"It's potato potahto you flying pain in my arse, and... I can't believe I'm actually having this conversation with you. Mother forging your private investigator license was bad enough, now you want to be armed?"

Mother said, "Hey now, Knith. I can run verification on her papers if you want."

I sputtered, "You're the one who wrote them so of course, you'll verify. I can't believe she talked you into one of her schemes. I thought you were supposed to be the most intelligent person on the world."

She reminded me, "I 'am' the world, Knith. And I like Graz, she talks to me like you do."

Graz chirped out with a smirk, "Stow it, you oversize tin can, I can fight my own battles."

I muttered to the air, "Children."

Then as we passed someone in a fleet support uniform floating past us with a gaping hole in his chest, blood globules trailing behind the Satyr, my eyes looked to the bulkhead reflexively. "Mother, can you raise Myra?"

The last I had heard from her, she had to leave our space convoy to round up the stray ships. That put her almost two hours out of position. And that's when they hijacked the Underhill. I was relieved when a familiar voice hissed then said in a distracted tone, "What's up, Fae lips? A little busy here." I heard an explosion as she cursed under her breath.

I was relieved she was still alive. "Oh, nothing, just taking a stroll in the Trunk. Just wanted to check up on you and your wingman."

She growled then said, "They lured me out of position, to where I was behind their main formation where their engine radiation was jamming my coms. When my scanners showed debris from Ready two, and what I thought was debris from the Underhill, just for the computers to identify them as bodies, I thought you were dead Knith. I couldn't warn the Leviathan because of how they had maneuvered me."

She sounded as if she blamed herself for everything. "Hey Kitty Cat, this was not your fault, they had fooled us all."

She muttered as I heard her pulse lasers firing, "It was a rookie mistake. Never leave your wingman."

Graz was repeating, "Hi Myra, hi Myra, hello Myra."

The woman responded, "Yes Graz, I hear you. Hello. Now, ladies, I've got some mutineers to mop up, stay safe."

My Sprite companion said, "Stay safe? I'm with Knith, she's charging right in on..."

"Goodbye and good luck, Myra." Mother cut the link.

I sighed and said, "She's ok." At the rate we were moving I still had two or three minutes before we reached the blast sphere and flight control. Then I asked, "Mother?"

She said, "Already connecting."

As much as I had worried about Myra, it had felt as if I had an anvil resting on my heart after I saw the damage to Beta-Stack's A-Ring and the hull breaches. I was a little occupied fighting for my life to find out if the woman who held my heart was ok.

"Knith? Oh, thank Mab you're ok. I heard the Underhill had docked with a boarding party. I feared the worst." She grunted and a huge amount of static filled the channel for a moment before she was panting and gasping. She called out to someone, "Ok, that should hold. Get me to the next one."

Then she said, "Just a second Knith, we'll lose coms during transport."

Transport? What did she... my thought was interrupted by heavy static then a spinning connection icon before the channel was clear, showing her location was no longer Beta A. She was in Gamma B now. She said, "Hang on Knith." Then she said, "I've got this, mother needs transport."

Then she was back with me as I heard magic crackling like it did when she was winding up her power to do something big. She said, "I have this last breach to seal. Titania has been transporting mother and me around through the entire attack. Ready Squadron says they are just mopping up some strangler ships. They are babbling about some sort of doomsday weapon that was batting the enemy from the sky."

She grunted and there was static. Then she was yelling, "That won't hold long, get those blast doors operational and get the people out of their quarters now that we have an atmosphere."

Then she was back with me. "I was so worried. And..." I heard her winding up again.

I found I was smiling and I said, "Well it sounds like you're a little busy. I have a little something I have to do to, so how about dinner?"

"Sounds delightful. Be careful."

Graz chuckled. "Careful? She's hunting the ringleader of the Outliers now, alone. And..."

I made a zipping motion over her lips then blurted, "Love you, Rory."

She responded in a tone full of suspicion. "Love you too, Knith Shade of Beta-Stack C-Ring."

Mother closed the channel and I reached about to drag a hand on the handrail until we slowed enough for me to lower my feet to the deck and let the mag-boots clomp down on the deck. The blast sphere that housed Mother's data core and flight control loomed ahead of us. The entire expanse of the huge corridor was tinged by a red mist that partially obscured the scene.

It took me a moment to realize what I was seeing. I heard my detached voice saying, "Gods."

And Graz turning her head away and saying, "I'm going to be sick." Then she spewed.

It was blood. A thick mist and floating globules of blood and carnage that made what we left behind look like a kindergarten party. Some of the corpses floating through the space were literally torn in half by what had to have been high powered weapons. There had to be at least thirty or forty Outlier bodies.

And against the bulkhead was a Megolith. One of its arms looked as if it had been chewed off... likely by sustained fire from one of those spinning projectile weapons. And there was a hole blown through its chest, the data overlay Mother was feeding me showed residue from some sort of chemical explosive. A spent EMP grenade was spinning lazily nearby.

I whispered, "Space me now... they had incapacitated him, then they tore him apart with their weapons even though he was helpless inside."

Graz growled, "These Outliers are nothing but animals. They don't see anyone who isn't Human as people, just as roaches to be exterminated."

I looked around scanning what looked to have been a one-sided battle until they used the EMP grenade to turn the tide. I was asking, "Where's the other..." when Mother highlighted something next to the blast doors. It was the other Megolith-Suit, on its back.

Running along the deck, I ignored the body parts and gore floating around us until we got up to the relatively intact suit. The main canon looked to have been melted somehow, more of that residue on it, and the access door to the pilot's rig was open, the pilot was missing.

I glanced at the blast door again. The driver would be cleared to raise the series of doors. They kept him alive to gain access to the blast sphere. How had they even gotten this far?

Stepping up to the door, I tried my bio scan and quantum encrypted codes. Access denied. I tried coms to warn our people in case the Outliers weren't as far ahead as I thought they were, "Flight Control, this is Shade, badge alpha three four eight niner. Come in? You have incoming hostiles."

Mother said softly, "Knith..." Then showed me a live feed of the control room. There was a battle raging in there as I watched.

I pounded on the door in frustration, then remembered Rory's magic overriding the door. I put my face right in front of the access terminal. The blew gently across my lips. Magic started to light on the runes for a few feet around the access pad, then receded. I punched the door in frustration, the magic wasn't powerful enough.

Then in a moment of inspiration, my eyes darted down to my gear pouches and I jammed my hand into one, feeling around until my hands closed around a piece of cool metal. I pulled it out and looked at the spelled harmonica Mac had given me in what seems another lifetime ago. It had amplified Mab's magic to help me stop Lord Sindri.

My hands shook as I brought it to my mouth. Then I blew out a solid, silvery, perfect note that seemed to shake reality around us, fire and ice exploded from the instrument, twisting and twirling around each other like the dance of long lost lovers as the magic amplified by an order of magnitude, then hit the access pad.

The silver traces of magic glowed brightly around the entire mammoth blast sphere, highlighting runes and spellwork so fine it could only have been made by the Queens of Fairie. Then the huge door rumbled open.

I looked inside, then back at the Megolith-Suit. I smirked and climbed up the suit and slid in. As soon as I settled in, the cockpit reconfigured for my size as neural contacts connected all around my armor.

I clenched my fist and the suit mimicked the motion. I just thought about it and the damaged weapon jettisoned. The up-time read only five minutes. The systems had just come back online, likely after an EMP shutdown. The auxiliary weapons systems were down, probably fried when the main weapon had. I stood and felt ten feet tall and powerful.

I slammed a giant metal fist into the other metal hand and said, "I can work with this." With a thought, the cockpit sealed. And I started moving forward on thrusters. It was as simple as thinking about it. I smirked, Titania's panties, I was piloting a Megolith!

We started forward as three men stepped out from behind one of the nearby vehicles, their heavy projectile weapons starting to spin up. Graz growled out in a cold tone, "Go, Knith, stop Richter, I got these steaming piles of fairy droppings."

I just inclined my head as the suit did the same, then the thrusters fired, moving me swiftly inside toward the next blast door as the screams started. I didn't look back.

Chapter 14 – Birthright

Door after door I had to open the cockpit access door to play a note on the harmonica. And I finally reached the inner blast door and inhaled a shaky breath, wincing from the sharp ache from my ribs that it caused. This was it. I played the note, then sealed the cockpit, clenching my fists in anticipation.

I flew to the relative ceiling, using the door for cover for as long as I could, and when it was halfway open, I had the Megolith-Suit swoop down and through the opening, its chest sparking on the deck plates. The shocked looks on the Outliers faces that were standing in front of the blast door, with the barrels of their heavy guns already spinning, told me that a Megolith was the last thing they expected to come through the doors.

That second of surprise was all I needed as I swung both arms forward, the suit's arms taking up a third of the entire opening as they slammed into the two men, shattering their weapons and sending the two men flying through the space to hit a console with a wet sounding impact followed by a spray of sparks.

"Hello, boys."

Mother was feeding me multiple views of the room from every angle, and bile rose in my throat. Everyone in Flight control had been slaughtered. From the guards at the door to the central core and K'Infinitum, to the Elvish Captain of the Leviathan, Prince J'Verris. The bastards had actually beheaded him.

I had to look away.

An oddly detached part of my mind was noting how Graz would be the first to point out that I had to work on my smack talk as half the Outliers remaining in the room, swinging weapons toward me were female.

I realized that I had somehow moved past rage to a place that scared the living hells out of me. I was to a point of calm and clarity. My mind pushed all emotion aside, knowing it could get me killed if I let it in. What was left? Well, what was left was a calculated killing machine that the Brigade has forged me into over the last two and a half decades. And I was about to bring the pain.

Richter, who was dragging a bloodied and beaten Minotaur in Enforcer armor through the air toward the inner door, was almost frothing at the mouth as he was screaming, "You! I should have killed you on the Underhill! Kill her now!" He was going to use the Megolith pilot to open the door.

My answer was not in words as the massive battle suit's feet magnetized and the room shook as I contacted the deck then charged the group who moved between me and him. Projectiles were ricocheting off the armor, and one heavier single-shot weapon that looked to almost knocking the woman holding it tore through the armor of the left arm. I realized it was a grenade launcher and she was readying another.

I leapt and cleared most of the group and just as I passed over her, fired the maneuvering thrusts in the shoulders of the suit and came down on her... well I came down on her like a two-ton Megolith, cutting her scream short as she realized this was her end.

I spun on the others. Mother had plots for nine hostiles in my vision so I could track them all as they circled me. I lashed out and sent a man slamming into the bulkhead. A red alarm icon bloomed and I spun to see a man raising a tube to his shoulder and before I could react, he pulled the trigger and a small rocket came shooting directly at my chest. I spun away, too late and then my ears were ringing as an explosion tore armor from the suit, setting off multiple systems failure alarms and damage reports scrolling in my head up.

So that's what they had used that destroyed a canon and left all that chemical explosive residue. I grabbed what looked to be the wreckage of a chair beside me and threw it at the man as he was sliding another of those rockets into the tube. It hit him hard, one of the mangled chair legs tearing through his vac-suit and his gut like it were tissue paper. He gasped as he spun toward the main displays thirty feet above the chair leg sticking out his back.

I was about to leap up to avoid the incoming fire when Richter hissed out, "EMP grenades you idiots! She'll be defenseless! They all rely on their superior tech, but without it they are nothing."

Three Outliers released their weapons to let them drift off and pulled those Titania be damned grenades out. My mind shot back to the image of the other Megolith pilot, how they had trapped him in his suit and just chewed a hole through the suit and him with their projectile weapons.

I shouted, "Mother!" And the access door jettisoned and the thrusters fired just as the three grenades went off. I had closed my eyes so the flash didn't temporarily blind me. Then I yanked myself through the opening down toward the deck, in my now unpowered armor.

They had gone overboard with the EMPs since the entire Flight Control Center was powered down. Only the emergency Fae-Light fixtures illuminated the space. Which meant Mother couldn't help me anymore until the systems rebooted, I was on my own.

Just before I hit the deck, I reached my boots and grabbed the manual bolts and shoved down, moving the magnets down. Then I hit the deck and the mag-boots engaged. Thank the foresight of the engineers to install the emergency manual controls in Brigade issue SAs just in case of suit failure. Though I'm sure they never anticipated having to use them this way after an EMP attack.

My legs took the impact since my servos were inoperable and I had to take a knee and slap the deck with my hands to absorb some of the kinetic energy. Then I looked up and smiled cruelly as they all just looked at me as I said through gritted teeth, "I don't need any tech to take out the trash."

Then I stood from my improvised three-point stance and charged them as Righter roared, "Shoot her!"

All the years of sparring with Enforcers of stronger and faster races have honed my own reflexes, and those same years of hand to hand combat drills had honed my skills and made them second nature, almost reflexive. I unleashed the weapon that the Brigade forged me into as muscle memory kicked in, in that odd calm I was still feeling.

They were spraying their weapons at me, but they weren't used to combat in a zero-G environment as the recoil from their weapons was pushing them back, causing them to overcompensate, compromising their aim.

My hands went to my hips and I drew my twin batons and snicked them out to full length as I closed the distance. A few projectiles struck, reminding me of my own injuries as I winced, but I didn't have time to let them slow me down.

I was spinning and kicking and striking out with the batons. Disarming first and disabling second. One woman was grabbing the discarded grenade launcher as I clotheslined a man and leapt at the bulkhead behind him then pushed off with all my better than normal Human strength and spun toward the woman, my fist cocked.

Just before she slammed a grenade into the weapon, I reached her, and I used all my momentum behind the best right hook I had ever thrown. That detached portion of my mind admired the woman's jaw distending then snapping before she was sent tumbling through the space. Then it noted that was about a nine-point five, half a point taken off for lack of witty taunt as the blow landed.

I dragged my toes until the magnets pulled me back to the deck, and I turned just to blurt out, "Argh," as something blew through the muscles of my left leg. A lucky shot had found a seam in the armor. Those joints were armored too when the suit was powered, but in power failure mode, this armor was like standard-issue Scatter Armor with articulation points, meaning seams and weak points.

I glanced around and realized that there was only one Outlier standing beside Richter. He was grinning as I dragged my leg behind me, blood globules spreading in the air. I prepared to dive aside when he pulled the trigger again... but nothing happened. He stared down at the weapon in horror, then grabbed it like a club and started for me.

He reached me, and faster than he could react as he hauled back to swing, I slammed both fists forward as I dove at him. They connected with his throat. I could hear and feel the cartilage crush under the assault, and I drifted past him as his eyes bulged wide while he grasped his throat, trying to draw in a breath that would never come.

Then I reached the bulkhead and reached out an arm as I panted and cushioned my arrival. I put my boots on the deck again and inhaled, pushing the pain away, and with it that cold detachment. It terrified me that I had such a cold, detached, and efficient killer living inside of me.

Then I turned slowly and glared at Richter. He and his Outlier fanatical doctrine had done that to me. They had made me deal out death again. Something I hoped I would never do again. And all that rage, and fear, and revulsion at what they had done fueled me. I bared my teeth at Richter where he stood at the door with the Minotaur as the systems all around us started blinking back to life.

"Let... him... go... Richter."

He shook his head and shoved a small version of the projectile weapons against the Minotaur's neck. "No. My Birthright is just beyond this door. Our cause, the Outlier's cause has come to fruition. We will claim control of the Worldship, of the people of the Worldship and claim what is rightfully ours. We will purge Humanity of the cockroaches that have enslaved them and we will take their place in power for all time. For Humankind!"

I sighed heavily as I kept walking toward him, dragging my leg, feeling a little faint from loss of blood, but I knew it would pass. My natural accelerated healing has probably already stemmed the bleeding. "I am so sick and tired of crazy people and their supervillain monologues like we are living in some bad mystery wave. This ends one of two ways, Richter, either you surrender your weapon and be bound by law, or you die here, a traitor to all the peoples of the world and the Cityships."

He shook his head and yelled at the Minotaur, "Place your hand on the access panel... NOW!"

He looked at the man with hate and rage, and the big enforcer said to me, his eyes boring into the crazy man, "Take him down, Shade. I won't let him use me to aid in his ethnic cleansing."

I started to yell, "No!" at him, but his hand had already shot up, encasing both Richter's hand and the gun and he squeezed hard, causing Richter's finger to pull the trigger... and the Minotaur went limp. I whispered in shock, "No..." He sacrificed himself, but he didn't need to. Richter was beaten.

I grabbed my MMGs, but they were still dead so I tossed them aside. Then I reached out to a floating body of an Outlier and grabbed the projectile weapon in its hands and swung it toward the Captain before he could gather his wits and aim his at me.

My finger had already pulled the trigger back halfway when, in an explosion of heated magic tinged with an icy fire, Mab and Titania appeared on either side of the man, grabbing his arms. Mab said to me, "Don't, child," as she wrenched over a hand, snapping Richter's arm like a twig, his weapon floating away as he screamed in agony.

For a long eternity, my finger held, instinct telling me that just a hair's breadth more and the weapon would fire. He was in my sights. Titania looked at me too, her eyes filled with sorrow for... me? And I dropped the weapon, watching it float away from me, and then I took a deep breath.

The man started to struggle again and was about to go into another tirade, but Mab just looked at him and an ice gag covered his mouth.

They turned away from me and Titania reached out and placed her hand on the access pad. The ribbons of magic shout out across the door again and it started to rise. I asked dumbly as I started limping forward, my voice hoarse, "What are you doing?"

Mab smiled back at me, chilling me to the bone as she said sweetly, her mannerism like a snake poised to strike, "We're giving him what he wants. The worm wants the Ka'Infinitum? Then the Ka'Infinitum he shall have."

With that, the man calmed and madness raged in his wide eyes, a contrast to the calm and reasonable man we had met upon arriving at the Redemption. He was smiling maniacally now, did he think he had won or something? The man didn't realize just how cruel the Queens could be. There's a reason there are so many cautionary tales about them. There were no happy stories about anyone meeting one of the Ladies of the divided courts.

They pulled the man through the door. I dragged myself after them, and absently kissed my hand and placed it on the sleek console in Mother's data core as we passed. Then they opened the chamber housing the artifacts of power.

I paused at the door, bathed in light when they dragged the man inside. I couldn't face the light of creation itself again. It had almost undone me the first time, and I still couldn't comprehend exactly what I had seen and experienced in that room. A sense of self-preservation or more specifically preservation of self wouldn't allow me to proceed any farther. The memory alone had tears flowing down my cheeks.

They released the man as he stared gape jawed into the light of the artifacts, seeing this small portion of the light of creation, of magic itself. He fell to his knees in whatever false gravity the Queens were providing, and he whispered, "My birthright. I have won..."

And I could sense what was left of his mind cracking at what he was seeing as he just started to laugh, softly as his skin started flaking away, drifting like ash in a breeze with the waves of magic flowing from the Ka'Infinitum. Then he was just gone before his eerie, disembodied laughter finished echoing off the walls.

And I felt... nothing.

Turning, I started back toward the Flight Center as I felt my armor finally start to power up its systems again. I hissed in pain as it clamped down on my leg and synth-skin patches were applied to my wounds. The red ready lights of Mother's cameras started to glow on the walls.

I hesitated, not looking back when Mab called out to me, "What? No admonition, Knith Shade of Beta-Stack C? No threats of binding us by law?"

Still not looking back, I said in a flat tone, "The man was dead the moment the Leviathan made contact with the Cityships. You were just the tools he used to commit his suicide."

I was met with a few heartbeats of silence, then I felt the surge of Summer magic as they teleported away.

Staggering, I made my way back into Flight Control and sat against the wall and slid down since my adrenaline had finally crashed on me and I didn't have the strength to move anymore. Mother was in my ear again, causing me to smile, realizing how much I missed her in my head the past few minutes.

She was babbling things about injuries, help coming, and that the world was secure. I just patted the wall, staring off at nothing as I waited. I was so finished with this day.

Epilogue

Delphine checked my armor and I her Mithreal as the Tug started firing reaction thrusters to slow us as we arrived at the Cityships.

She and Captain Yar's frozen, but still very much alive, bodies had been retrieved from space at the far range of Ready Squadron, they had drifted past the world when the battle began and Mother had them painted with lidar the entire time. And once the Worldship was secure, Myra herself went out on retrieval. It had almost been too late. As it was she had run out of fuel on the way back, and other fighters from the squadron met her halfway to transfer fuel.

So of course, after they thawed, Delphine and Yar had been the first to volunteer for the liberation boarding party fleet we were sending to the Cityships to root out the rest of the Outlier mutineers.

I looked out the front windows at the frightening sight of the one hundred and fifty-three ready squadron fighters escorting our ten maintenance tugs on the short journey to the Cityships that were just twenty-four hours from falling into formation beside the Leviathan. We were going to flush out the mutineers and secure the Cityships and their people before any other attacks could be made against the world.

It still surprised me how quickly Operation Liberation had come together, even while legions of repair crews swarmed the Worldship, and standby crews were assigned to Flight Control. When Rory finally let me out of bed the morning after the battle, all critical systems that were damaged during the attack were operational. The only thing that was going to take weeks or more was all the hull damage and the damage to the sky structure.

Never in the history of the world had the mammoth isolation gates been extended from the lower bulkhead levels to the overhead sky structure because of a breach in the transparent armor panels in the open space of a ring.

But Alpha and Beta's rings were the hardest hit, directly over the Summer and Winter palaces. They knew exactly what they were doing, but the biggest failing of the Outliers was that they didn't understand magic, as they have never witnessed it.

And when Rory brought me home, bypassing Med-Tech, we had to go through some blast seal doors into the section of the ring that should have undergone full decompression, but hadn't. The portion of the honeycomb sky superstructure that had been torn away by the industrial mining lasers, was covered in coherent magic, blue shimmering ice stretching for hundreds of yards.

Aurora and Queen Mab had sealed the breaches before too much could be sucked out into space and too much damage could be done to the idyllic forests and rivers of the A-Ring. They expended more and more magic as Titania teleported them from breach to breach in all the Stacks. And even exhausted, my girl had spent the night healing me. And telling me over and over, "How extraordinarily foolish and reckless you are, Knith. Why must you charge into danger before you have backup?"

I had countered, "But I did have backup, Graz was there and you aren't chastising her."

"I'm not sleeping with her, and I assure you, I can hear her spouses chastising her as well."

Then she had huffed and said, "I love that you fight when others run and that you have the courage that sometimes overshadows your sense. But I've grown quite fond of you in my life and would be most cross if you were taken from me because you still choose to tilt at windmills."

Ah-ha! I knew that one now. She always accused me of that, so I had to find out the reference. I smirked. "Don Quixote."

She rolled her eyes. What? I thought I was clever finding a reference that was hundreds of thousands of years old. Ok, maybe I asked Mac and he happened to have an actual paper book about Don Quixote.

That thought of Mac had me hesitate before I asked, "How are you doing after... you know... Mac?"

She closed her eyes, calming herself and saying in a measured tone which told me she wasn't as ok as she pretended when she said, "I'm fine. We always thought he was hiding out around the world somewhere. It had always been unlikely that a wily old Fae like him would suffer some sort of untimely end while riding with his Wild Hunt."

I squinted an eye when she shoved more magic into my leg, a little roughly. "I'm sure... well I'm not sure he had a good reason, but I do know that he is a good man."

That was all we said on the subject. Well mostly because all my injuries, then having my girl's magic slapping me around to heal me had exhausted me beyond belief and I had just closed my eyes for a moment and when I woke it was morning.

Then I had to suffer through first Mab then Titania kissing me to reinforce their marks and having my princess shooing them away from our bed and threatening them quite impressively if they ever invaded my or her bedchambers again.

The old man hasn't docked the Underhill yet, but he did accept a call from Rory and even Mab a couple days later. The Underhill was out there somewhere in formation. I think Mac has a personal score to settle with Captain Vandross, and we couldn't forbid him to interfere since again, he was a Remnant captain and not under the purview of the laws of the world. Though a Human captain, he was not. Now that he has revealed his true nature, there was no going back for him.

All the news waves have been broadcasting footage of him slinging magical lightning on the Skin for days. All the headlines reading things such as, "Oberon returns in the world's darkest hour," and the like.

News of his return overshadowed the news of the Outlier attack, especially in the Fae communities.

I cringed at the footage of the idiot in front of him, charging a group of armed Outliers and three mining ships. I'm starting to think there might be something wrong with me. Graz disagrees, she says I'm, "An adrenaline junkie with an overdeveloped sense of right, you dumb Big."

As the cityships grew in the window, the commander of the fleet started squawking out demands for surrender. I looked to my shoulder where Graz sat in Mithreal armor and a Mithreal blade on her hip. I smirked at her. Mab had actually presented the armor to her for her acts of bravery in the battle and made her an honorary palace guard.

She started to ask, "So, palace guard. Can I get..."

"No. No, you can't have a miniature MMG made for you."

"Mab's tit's, Knith. You're no fun."

I told her as the Cityships now filled the windows as we started a precision roll to line up with an airlock as defiance crackled over the com channel, "Ok, now stay with me and follow the Commander's orders. Time to free these people."

She nodded staunchly as the ship shook slightly and the sound of docking clamps latching on echoed through the crowded ship. She growled out as orders started sounding over the intercom, "Let's do this, Knith."

Mother echoed the sentiment, determined anger in her tone, "I've got your back."

Smiling as my visor snicked into place while I drew my twin MMGs, I whispered, "You always do."

Then we headed out as I took a deep breath. After today, the world was never going to be the same.

The End

<u>Novels by Erik Schubach</u>

Books in the Worldship Files series...

Leviathan

Firewyrm

Cityships

Morrigan (2020)

Books in the Techromancy Scrolls series...

Adept

Soras

Masquerade

Westlands

Avalon

New Cali

Colossus (2020)

Books in the Urban Fairytales series...

Red Hood: The Hunt

Snow: The White Crow

Ella: Cinders and Ash

Rose: Briar's Thorn

Let Down Your Hair

Hair of Gold: Just Right

The Hood of Locksley

Beauty In the Beast

No Place Like Home

Shadow Of The Hook

Armageddon

Books in the New Sentinels series...

Djinn: Cursed

Raven Maid: Out of the Darkness

Fate: No Strings Attached

Open Seas: Just Add Water

Ghost-ish: Lazarus

Anubis: Death's Mistress
Sentinels: Reckoning (2020)

Books in the Drakon series...
Awakening
Dragonfall

Books in the Valkyrie Chronicles series...
Return of the Asgard
Bloodlines
Folkvangr
Seventy Two Hours
Titans

Books in the Tales From Olympus series...
Gods Reunited
Alfheim
Odyssey (2020)

Books in the Bridge series...
Trolls
Traitor
Unbroken
Krynn

Books in the Fracture series...
Divergence

<u>Novellas by Erik Schubach</u>
The Hollow

Novellas in the Paranormals series...
Fleas
This Sucks
Jinx (2020)

Novellas in the Fixit Adventures...
Fixit
Glitch
Vashon

Descent

Sedition (2020)

Novellas in the Emily Monroe Is Not The Chosen One series...

Night Shift

Unchosen

Rechosen (2020)

Short Stories by Erik Schubach

(These short stories span many different genres)

A Little Favor

Lost in the Woods

MUB

Mirror Mirror On The Wall

Oops!

Rift Jumpers: Faster Than Light

Scythe

Snack Run

Something Pretty

Romance Novels by Erik Schubach

Books in the Music of the Soul universe...

(All books are standalone and can be read in any order)

Music of the Soul

A Deafening Whisper

Dating Game

Karaoke Queen

Silent Bob

Five Feet or Less

Broken Song

Syncopated Rhythm

Progeny

Girl Next Door

Lightning Strikes Twice

June

Dead Shot
Music of the Soul Shorts...
(All short stories are standalone and can be read in any order)
Misadventures of Victoria Davenport: Operation Matchmaker
Wallflower
Accidental Date
Holiday Morsels
What Happened In Vegas?
Books in the London Harmony series...
(All books are standalone and can be read in any order)
Water Gypsy
Feel the Beat
Roctoberfest
Small Fry
Doghouse
Minuette
Squid Hugs
The Pike
Flotilla
Books in the Pike series...
(All books are standalone and can be read in any order)
Ships In The Night
Right To Remain Silent
Evermore
New Beginnings
Books in the Flotilla series...
(All books are standalone and can be read in any order)
Making Waves
Keeping Time
The Temp
Paying the Toll
Books in the Unleashed series...
Case of the Collie Flour

Case of the Hot Dog
Case of the Gold Retriever
Case of the Great Danish
Case of the Yorkshire Pudding
Case of the Poodle Doodle
Case of the Hound About Town
Case of the Shepherd's Pie
Case of the Bull Doggish

Don't miss out!

Visit the website below and you can sign up to receive emails whenever Erik Schubach publishes a new book. There's no charge and no obligation.

https://books2read.com/r/B-A-QJLI-EFUEB

BOOKS 2 READ

Connecting independent readers to independent writers.

Lightning Source UK Ltd.
Milton Keynes UK
UKHW010622141022
410433UK00002B/433

9 781393 228479